LOCKDOWN PHANTOM #2

Compiled & Edited by

D. Kershaw | Maggie Pawsey | S.N. Graves

Also available and coming soon from Black Hare Press

DARK DRABBLES ANTHOLOGIES

WORLDS

ANGELS

MONSTERS

BEYOND

UNRAVEL

APOCALYPSE

LOVE

HATE

OCEANS

ANCIENTS

BHP WRITERS' GROUP SPECIAL EDITIONS

STORMING AREA 51

EERIE CHRISTMAS

BAD ROMANCE

TWENTY TWENTY

OTHER VOLUMES

DEEP SPACE

WHAT IF?

KEY TO THE KINGDOM

DEEP SEA

BEYOND THE REALM

Twitter: @BlackHarePress

Facebook: BlackHarePress

Website: www.BlackHarePress.com

Cover Design	Dawn Burdett	www.dmburdett.com
Formatting	Ben Thomas	www.blackharepress.com
Editing	D. Kershaw	www.blackharepress.com
	Maggie Pawsey	
	S.N. Graves	www.sngraves.com
Read Team	David Green	davidgreenwritercom.wordpress.com
	Jennifer Hatfield	jhatfieldauthor.wixsite.com/website
	Jodi Jensen	jodijensenwrites.wordpress.com
	Lyndsay Ellis-Holloway	authorlyndseyellisholloway.webador.co.uk
	Stacey Jaine McIntosh	www.staceyjainemcintosh.com

TABLE OF CONTENTS

GHOST SHIP

By McKenzie Richardson

The blue-tinged outline of a ship appeared beneath the waves, raising the hairs on the back of his neck. Rationally, he knew it was just an old shipwreck, the poor souls drowned and gone. But still, the way it seemed to glow in the darkness just below the surface, like a ghost ship waiting to carry passengers to the afterlife.

He rolled his eyes at his own imagination. From behind him, he heard a muffled thud and whirled around to see his first mate sprawled out on the deck. The captain helped the man to his feet.

"Are you alright?" he asked. The first mate's face was white as the moon. "You look as though you've seen a ghost."

The mate stared just beyond the captain's left ear, eyes wide, chin trembling, unable to speak.

The captain didn't even have time to turn.

OLD JACK

By Callum Pearce

Old Jack had been a resident of his current home for as long as he could remember. The house had seen great family feasts and parties that lasted into the next day. It had seen drama, love, and laughter.

Sometimes the house seemed to remember even more than Old Jack did. Just touching the walls, you could feel the beat of the music played in one room or feel the thud of crockery smashing against walls in another. Every moment of the lives shared here left a small echo. Even camera crews and celebrities had passed through the old painted front door over the years. Priests and preachers of every type had come here to this place, all to visit Old Jack.

Now he had to watch people traipsing through the house as though he wasn't there. They'd walk around talking about what fixtures and fittings could be salvaged before they knocked the place down, taking with it all of those old echoes. The last people to pay any attention to Old Jack had been the first family he had haunted. Decades ago now, he dreamed about playing with those girls again. He loved to lift them and throw them from one bed to another. When witnesses were there, the girls would pretend to be terrified. They would build up the drama for anyone who cared to see it. When witnesses were gone, they would roll around the floor laughing together. Jack missed the musical sound of their laughter.

Jack didn't remember when the first family had arrived. There seemed to be a few decades missing in his memory. He struggled to find anything between when he had died and when he first started interacting with the family in his old home. In fact, he only remembered small parts of his life when the girls told stories about him. Each story they told opened a new door in his memory and shone a light on part of his life. When he started to become aware of his surroundings, he remembered being shocked by the decoration of the place since it had been his home. The Eighties had brought a taste for lots of clashing colours. Some rooms would even share the same loud brash pattern between the wallpaper, curtains, and the couch. The memories of his old life seemed quite grey in comparison. The old place had that he used to live in had now been filled with colour and sound, playthings lay everywhere, for adults and children alike.

When he had first become aware of the family, his home was filled with anger and pain. A drunken father stomped around the house looking for any reason to explode. The mother worked as a slave and the two daughters entertained themselves in their rooms. When their father was away, the girls were happy and playful. They loved to play tricks on each other, making up stories and playing games. They even told stories about him. His mind would fill with memories as the girls talked about his old life. He had no idea how they knew so much about him.

Eventually, their mother had had enough, and he was booted out of the house. She found herself working every day to provide for her girls. The girls grew restless with the lack of attention. Jack tried to soothe them and tell them stories at night-time. Whilst it seemed that they didn't hear him, they both continued to tell each other stories about him. The old man that haunted their house. They would play tricks on each other and blame him, make noises in the night to scare their mother. It was always Old Jack to blame. He didn't mind; he liked that they wanted to play. He felt less lonely with Jane and Ellie including him in their games.

The girls found that their games and stories of Old Jack brought them more attention than they had ever hoped for. They screamed and giggled as he threw them each from one bed to the other. They constantly irritated their mother with stories. It was only when they started to wake up with scratches on their body that their mother decided to look for help. Jack didn't even remember scratching them until they told their mother about it. He didn't understand why he had done it, except maybe to get them more attention. First, they were taken to doctors. Next, they were introduced to priests. Then came the television cameras, scientists, and psychics, competing to tell Old Jack's story to the world.

The psychics would roam the house, stopping in each room to tell a small part of his story. They talked of his son and his wife. Sometimes, the girls would step in with titbits of their own. It always hurt to hear them talking about his family. He often wondered why he had been left here to haunt his old home, whilst they had seemingly moved on to another place. When he listened to the psychics and the girls telling his tale, he could remember their faces vividly. He missed them so much and longed to find them again someday. For some reason, he had been left here. Jack decided he would make the best of it with his new family whilst he had them. Irene had found, to her surprise, that she, too, liked the attention Old Jack was bringing to the home. They would all sit around the small television in the evening watching themselves talking to the interviewers that had passed through the house. Irene even started to talk to Old Jack herself, when nobody was around, and she had things to get off her chest.

People would crowd around outside

the house hoping to get a glimpse of Old Jack. Sometimes they would swear they had caught him in a photograph, and then they, too, would appear on the small television, making themselves part of his story. The clothes people wore when they visited seemed like fancy dress to a man from Jack's time. Men with painted faces and coloured hair lined up outside taking photos. Women in brightly coloured, incredibly revealing clothes would gather too. He loved to watch them chatting and laughing as they hoped to be scared by the famous ghost.

The mood changed quite suddenly. At first, the family was celebrated, but slowly Jack noticed a different tone to the interviews. They asked questions about the girl's father, by now a quite well known angry drunk that caused lots of problems in their small town. Then they started to show videos where they suspected they had caught the girls trying to cheat the film crews. Ellie scratching her arm in the background of one scene, then screaming. Jane throwing something across the room and then overreacting for the cameras. He felt awful as he watched these people rip his new family apart. Every defence the family offered up only served to alienate people further. Now, people turned up outside to throw stones or drop litter in their garden. People shouted abuse from the pavement outside his house. The psychics on the television screen made their excuses for being duped by his dishonest family.

Their moment of fame over, the girls didn't seem to want to play with Old Jack anymore. Irene went back to working all day and sleeping through the evenings, and eventually, people stopped turning up outside. Jack felt lonelier than ever before, longing to move on to wherever his wife and son had gone. The old ghost hated himself for bringing so much trouble to his adopted family. He wished he could prove his existence and remove their shame and sadness. At the same time, he worried that anything he may do would only bring them more trouble. He hadn't predicted what would happen last time and didn't want to do anything to hurt the girls again. Jack spent the next five years watching over his family quietly, never doing anything more than whisper kind words to them as they lay in bed at night. He hoped they could hear him, even though they gave no sign.

After five years, Jack noticed the girls and their mother had started appearing on the flickering television screen again. The passing of time had brought a renewed interest in the family. People started contacting them to do more interviews about that time in their life and what had happened since. At first, they resisted, but so much money was being offered, Irene decided to do one interview for a television show. She hoped that she could clear her family's name and then move on from the whole affair. He started to see commercials on the television, promising to find out what had happened to the haunted family of Grange Road. They showed old clips of the girls five years ago and the crowds who had gathered around the house. He was worried that things may go as they had before, but part of him was excited too.

Suddenly, his house was full of people again. The equipment they brought with them was different from the things they had used the first time around. People milled about, setting up lights and screens. Cameras on stands sat all around the front room. Some people walked around with smaller cameras, filming the rooms where everything had happened. The family was nervous but hoped that this would be the last time they would have to do this. They wanted to make it clear that they hadn't been lying, that clips had been taken out of context and assumptions had been made. They wanted to tell people how hurt their family had been by the outpouring of hatred they had all experienced. How changed their lives had been by the disgust and distrust of their neighbours. Jack hoped the psychics would come again and tell his story for the world. He missed the vivid memories their tales of his life would bring. He missed his wife and son.

The interview started well enough. Irene and the girls sat in the living room calmly answering the interviewer's questions. He asked about their experiences in the house and how they had felt with the press intrusion into their lives. The interviewer gave them a chance to put forward their argument about how they were treated and how it had affected them.

"Can we talk about Paul Jones?" The interviewer leaned towards the family with his microphone.

"I'm sorry, I don't understand," Irene stammered.

"The psychic?" she asked.

"Yes, you may have seen on our program that we recently reported on his death."

"I'm sorry to hear that. He always seemed very kind."

"He died penniless and alone after the tricks your family played on him." The interviewer's tone had changed completely. "I mean, we've just sat here for half an hour listening to how awful it all was for your family. I wonder if you have any words about what you did to that poor man?" Irene and the girls stared blankly at the interviewer. "You can imagine it was quite hard for him to get work after being famously linked to the big con you played on the country."

"We didn't con anybody," Irene mumbled. "We didn't choose for any of this to happen."

"Oh, come on," the interviewer sneered.

"The girls were seen on camera carrying out this ridiculous game. They fed him parts of the story so that he could embarrass himself on television."

"My girls were frightened of whatever was in this house."

"Was!" The interviewer jumped on the word.

"So it isn't here anymore? When did it go? About the same time as the reporters stopped turning up I would imagine. Just as soon as the money dried up, hey?"

Old Jack watched the girls and their mother squirming on the couch. Each question seemed to cut them deeper. He was disgusted by the ambush that had been enacted upon his family and hated the smug attitude of the interviewer. He spoke as though he had a personal grudge against the family. As though their time in the spotlight had personally hurt him.

"So, no words for the man you drove to a miserable death, then?"

This was too much for Jack. He ran to

the middle of the room and threw the small coffee table up into the air. It crashed against the wall as the interviewer and Jack's adopted family all jumped out of their seats. Pushing the couch over so that it rested on its back, he turned to the frightened interviewer. He swung as though to hit him in the face, but his hand went right through the man. Somehow he seemed to make contact with the camera, which fell to the floor, smashing into pieces. People were already frantically packing things away as pictures fell from the walls all around the room. The interviewer who had seemed so confident when attacking three women was out the door before any of the others. Jack laughed hard as the frightened bullies rushed outside, filling their van with the equipment. The interviewer returned briefly, promising to arrange another time to see them, somewhere other than the house. He reminded them that they had a contract to fulfill, in case they had changed their mind about taking part in his program.

As soon as the van had driven away, Irene and the girls quickly packed as much as they could and left the house. Jack was sorry that he had gone so far, but at least now people would know the girls weren't liars. At least his family could let go of the shame that he had caused them. Even if it meant he would never see them again. People came with a van and slowly emptied everything from the house to take wherever his family had gone. He missed the girls almost as much as he had missed his own family. He only hoped that one day he would be with them all again.

*****

The house stayed empty for a few years. Jack had nothing to do but dwell on his pain and regret. He longed to hear anything about the girls and wished he would go to wherever his wife and son were waiting for him. He felt as though he was in hell. Forced to stay in an empty house, never knowing what became of either of his families.

Eventually, a new family moved into the house. A mother and father with their two sons. The patterned wallpaper was replaced with light pastel shades, the television they brought with them was so much bigger than he had ever seen before. Everything was different, but at least his house was full again. The boys didn't play with him or talk to him, but he enjoyed the sound of them playing and laughing together. He imagined his son running and playing with them. He hoped that wherever his son was, the sun shone, and he was able to play. Jack still moved things like toys around the house to amuse himself. People just assumed they had put their things down in the wrong place and moved them back.

Sometimes, people still stopped outside the house, forming small groups, taking photos. They would usually be chased away by one of the family members. The clothes had changed to ripped denim and t-shirts. They held gadgets and had wires permanently hanging from their ears. Some had metal in their faces, piercing their lips, nose, or eyebrows. The world kept changing around Old Jack. He imagined showing his wife and son this strange new world that he was witnessing. They would look at him like an experienced time traveller, an expert on this new age. He would never let them know that he was just as lost as them.

Old Jack watched his new family grow up. Eventually, one of the boys started to bring women home. The other started to bring men home. Each set out into the world in adult relationships, leaving their parents behind. When they visited, he was as excited to see them as their real parents were, even though they were completely unaware of him. When the father died in his bed, Jack watched closely for any sign of where his spirit went. Would he be trapped here like Jack, or did he go on to heaven or hell? There was no sign of anything leaving the old man's dead body. Nobody joined Jack in limbo. The mother moved out to live with one of the boys, and the house was emptied again for another family.

A single mother and her son came next. Jack tried everything to get their attention. His loneliness was becoming unbearable. He shouted and wailed, he banged pipes all night. He moved things from place to place. The family heard none of his wails. They tidied away the things he moved, and they called plumbers to deal with the pipes. When they left, the house stayed empty. People came and talked about pulling it down. The whole street was to be leveled to make way for new homes. Cheaper, cleaner, newer homes. What would become of Old Jack?

Would he stay here on this spot when the new buildings rose, or would he leave with the last brick of his home? He pictured himself haunting a pile of rubble, permanently connected to the remains of his old house. He hoped that the destruction of his place would free him at last from this world. He imagined his wife and son with their arms open to welcome him. He would have so much to tell them about the world they had left behind. The fashions, the gadgets, the painted men and women of the future. They would hang on his every word as he told them about the families he had watched grow in their old home. They would fill with pride as he regaled them with tales of his time as the famous ghost of Grange Road.

One day, as he waited for the house to be destroyed, the door swung open and the house started to fill with people. It was television people again. The equipment had changed, but he recognized the setup. They set up cameras and monitors, draped cloths over the fixtures and fittings. Then, they brought in large lights on stands but filled the room with dripping candles as well. He assumed this was to create a spooky atmosphere. When everything was set up, a familiar face arrived at the door. The interviewer from all those years ago was here again. His face was so much older but still recognizable. He had been a boy of about twenty years the first time, filled with the confidence of a much older man. Now his face matched his demeanour more. His attitude didn't seem to have changed much at all.

"What time are the old girls getting here?" he asked a nervous-looking assistant.

"They're on their way. We should be able to get started in an hour or so."

"Okay, let's get an intro done. Get those candles lit."

The interviewer talked into a camera. He spoke of the girls who had once lived here and the attention that swirled around them. He explained that after his interview with them years ago, the family had disappeared. They had stayed away from the press and changed their names. They had lived a modest and happy life out of the spotlight. Now though, they had decided to come out of the shadows, do one last interview in their old home before the place was finally pulled down.

Jack wanted to jump for joy or cry or punch the air. His emotions were everywhere. His girls were coming home to see him one last time. He'd never needed to change his clothes, but he felt as though he should be dressing in his smartest attire whilst he waited. The hour dragged on, seeming so much longer. The television people recorded small clips around the house. Then came a knock at the door. Old Jack fidgeted excitedly as the interviewer led the girls, now old women, into the room and helped them to get comfortable on the seats they had set up. The girls didn't seem to see Old Jack at first but he watched and waited patiently.

When everybody was comfortable and the cameras were rolling, the interviewer turned a small screen toward the women.

"I wanted to start with a small clip of the last interview I did with you here. Usually, we would cut away to it, but I'd actually like you to watch this with me."

The girls turned to the screen as the interview played.

"Now this is where things got quite

strange. I must admit you had me scared at the time."

Jack watched as the table flipped up on the screen and the people started jumping up and rushing around.

"Technology has moved on a lot since those days," the interviewer continued.

"See, now we can do this."

The scene played again only this time the image slowly zoomed in to the girl's feet. Jack watched as Ellie kicked the table hard into the air. This couldn't be. He remembered lifting the table and throwing it himself. Then he saw Jane pushing the couch onto its back when everybody was distracted looking at the table. When the couch hit the wall, pictures fell from the nails that held them. The picture zoomed again, to show her foot pulling at a wire on the floor as one of the cameras crashed down. Jack shook his head in disbelief. The video must have been somehow altered by the devious interviewer.

"That's why we wanted to do this interview," Ellie spoke softly.

"You made it all up, didn't you?" The interviewer spat the words out in disgust.

The girls nodded, and Jack's head swam. None of this was right. The girls slowly explained how they would throw things when people weren't looking. They showed the interviewer how they used to sit on their folded leg so that they could push themselves up into the air, as though thrown by invisible hands. They explained how one sister would distract whoever was viewing them and the other would move things around or make noises. He couldn't believe what he was hearing. It had never occurred to him that he may just be a figment of the girls' overactive imagination.

"The psychics used to make up stories of his past, so we just added in bits of the story ourselves. It seemed like a game."

Jack felt dizzy and lost. He knew straight away that it was all true. Every memory of his life and afterlife had come from their stories. If they said he did something, it became part of his memories. He had only started thinking of his wife and son when he had heard the girls and the fake psychics improvising his history. He had mourned them ever since. A family that never existed outside of their made-up tales. The two girls that he had missed for all of these years had played the cruellest trick on him that anybody ever could. They made him mourn people that weren't real. They had made him wait all of these years, longing to feel an embrace that would never come. His family and himself were only ever a cry for attention from two selfish little girls.

The girls didn't need their bag of tricks this time. Whatever he had been to begin with was not who he was now. He existed independently of the two girls. He had thoughts and feelings. What had started as a story, with the extra energy his rage brought him, was now becoming very real indeed. He could feel a strength building within him, burning like the pain he felt. Jack was ready to show them all what he could do.

The door slammed shut with a bang that echoed around the old house. He flung the camera equipment and monitors against the wall. People rushed to escape the building, but as the girls got to the door, he slammed it again, trapping them and the bemused interviewer in the room. The girls rushed to the other door, but that slammed shut too. Jack shoved the candles over, and flames started to spread quickly through the dusty, old room. They burned the material that had been draped around the place for the atmosphere, then the screens that separated parts of the room.

The interviewer pulled frantically at

one of the doors and the girls tried hard to open the other to no avail. As the flames and smoke filled the room, the girls held each other tight and sobbed. Old jack made sure that the last thing they saw, as the flames licked their clothes and the smoke filled their lungs, was his angry face, staring through the fire. They would never understand the pain they had caused him. That somewhere in their games and stories, they had created a real, thinking, feeling thing. In his last moments, he tried to hold on to the implanted memories of his imaginary family. As the three trapped people died, Jack slowly faded from a world he had never truly belonged in.

WINGS OF DEATH

By Zoey Xolton

Silently I come, no more than a shadow, a whisper in the night. I slink through the village on skeletal wings, seeking the one called Evette. When I find her, she is waiting for me. I drift into her home, past her herbs, hexes, and rings of salt.

"I am ready," says the witch with quiet defiance.

I admire her courage. Not all fear death, *but most fear the Reaper*. "You have not fulfilled your blood debt, and the Devil would have his due."

"So be it." She closes her eyes, smiling, as I cleave her soul from her flesh.

First published in *Curses & Cauldrons* - Blood Song Books, 2019

PIN THE BUNNY

By D.J. Elton

Chloe looked at the Easter bunny Robert had gifted her on the Thursday before the long weekend. It was a thin, colourless thing with a pouchy face, and long floppy legs.

"This will do," she thought, as she sorted through her pin-box for a thimble and sharp tiny scissors. Sitting at the kitchen table, she held the bunny on her knees. A red-top pin for the heart. "He can't do this to me," she said, aware of the buckets of tears she had cried in the past two days. Limp bunny got a sharp jab.

A blue-top pin for each thigh. "He won't be able to move." She smirked. "He won't be able to touch her." Four black-top pins, one for each hand and the top side of his shoulders.

"He will be tortured by his desires." Two yellow-top pins to each temple and a third between the eyes at the nose bridge.

That will do just fine. Gloatingly, she prided herself on the pin colour and body combinations. In moments she felt sickness in her belly when remembering how Robert had told her, with moist eyes, that he had to spend the Easter weekend with his team on the Gold Coast, to plan out the company's next six months. Robert must take her for a complete fool. Chloe knew he was going for a rendezvous with his assistant, that young attractive girl, whose text messages and risqué photos she had seen when she trolled his phone. It was no surprise. *Just cruel and thoughtless*. She was seven months pregnant, which he had seemed to have forgotten.

Chloe smiled wickedly to herself. She would have a good night's sleep. Some Easter bunny voodoo would pay them back. The news would come fairly fast, and she couldn't wait. Revenge was delicious.

POULS LIFE

By Christopher T. Dabrowski
Translated by Julia Mraczny

Paul is an obese jerk. She's bored with him.

I'll change it.

I've made his athletic friend Bartek see her.

He notices her. They like each other.

Paul understands that he's lost her.

He decides to change.

I point him to the flyer about an open week at the gym.

I help him discover his passion.

I'm his guardian angel. I'm him, but I've died in the future as a fulfilled man.

The soul knows no barriers. I came back to help myself live a better life.

Fortunately, he listens to his intuition. Otherwise, I would not have a chance.

BRUSH YOUR TEETH

By Galina Trefil

Tamara shivered as, over the high-pitched squeal of the dental drill, growling and clawing sounds menaced from all sides of the room.

Oh, how she'd begged her Mommy not to make her come here! Everyone knew this had once been the town morgue. "It's haunted," the dentist would even chortle to his paediatric patients. Kids knew it was no joke. They'd seen the terrible, angry shadows creeping up behind him as he dug away at their cavities.

Tamara whimpered as cold, invisible fingertips touched her neck.

"You'll start brushing your teeth now, huh?" The dentist snickered.

How right he was.

PURGATORY

By Ximena Escobar

The shovel was nearly as big as Ben, but he didn't want to wait for his father. I kept shouting at him that he was going to hurt his back, but he knew to spread his hands apart and eventually managed to dig a hole; no sign of the wood pigeon, though.

"It's not here!" Ben shouted from the other side of the pond, the shovel still in his hand.

He'd swaddled the headless bird in his Ronaldo shirt, much to my dismay; but since the footballer's then-recent theatrics on the pitch, he didn't care for it anymore. Never one to forgive easily, old Ben. Even at such a young age. I knew that about him.

"Could a fox have dug it out?" I shouted back.

Ben shook his head. He hadn't acknowledged me once until then, confirming he could hear me all along.

"Do they do that? Or do they only hunt live things?"

He just kept staring at the vacant hole,

ignoring me. (*That nastiness in him.* I understood his anger, but that didn't mean I deserved it.)

"You sure that's the spot?" (I knew it was. I'd seen him remove the markings before he started digging, but I asked anyway.) "Maybe the earth's already digested the bones?"

Ben didn't answer, bending over to pick up the white bundle behind him. One of my tea towels this time. A hedgehog he'd found on his way back from school, which he wanted to lay beside the pigeon for company. I watched him place it carefully in the empty grave, contemplate it in silence before filling the hole with dirt. I wanted to hold his hand, have him feel my presence beside him during this sadness—

a calm, reassuring presence such as a mother's should be, unlike the stunt I'd pulled during the pigeon situation. But the ground separating us was bumpy and uneven, still soft after the night's rain. And Ben wouldn't help, he'd only spread the mud all around the house, and I'd want to kill myself. I waited. I waited to hug him when he came.

But he hadn't been crying. At nine I'd have bawled my eyes out about a baby hedgehog dying, but I'd seen no tears when he first arrived with it from school, only an enthusiasm to deal with the problem like a man—and I saw no tears then. I used to cry every time a horse died on the telly; hurt me more than when the men were killed. Ben only said, "It's not real, mum," and then went off to play, shooting at enemies or deer from behind the furniture.

"Come here," I offered, watching him drag the shovel along the grass.

He came matter-of-factly, the blade hurting my teeth as he stepped onto the concrete. He didn't put his arms around me but stopped beside me for a moment, like a fleeting cheek-to-cheek, disappearing a second later.

It dawned on me the moment for hugs was past, those hugs like we used to share, where I was bigger and he smaller. Not a real dawning because I already knew this; but the notion always surged like a new day, cold and cruel as fresh water always is when you're dry, no matter how many times you've stepped in it, nor how accurately you can predict it will feel. Pigeons rustled the trees; a cat ran out from under the car. Squirrels squirreled along the fence, and dark clouds glided across the white sky, covering me with Ben's absence like it was new, the world around me always the voice of my intuition, a soundtrack, an extension of my body. Like now that I couldn't conquer the world, it conquered me instead. Like it and I were the same.

I pressed my button and turned, wheeling myself up the ramp and into the house. I didn't have to run over the shovel, he'd left it leaning against the wall, but I still expected to find a mess everywhere.

"Ben?

I looked for his shoes, scanned the

floor for dirt, but other than his rucksack and coat, I saw nothing. Only the drawer he'd left open when he got the tea towel.

Maybe he'd wiped his feet on the doormat and put them in the shoe rack? It hadn't occurred to me to check. (Maybe he'd turned a corner. Maybe now was the time for a fresh start for us. More sharing, less me nagging him. Maybe we could get along now, if I wasn't upset all the time.)

"Ben? Come talk to me. Would you like anything?"

Hot chocolate usually did the trick, but as my hearing stretched and lingered in the silence outside his bedroom door, I remembered he made his own these days, helped himself to the pantry when he wanted. I thought of what I could cook for him, but of course, Tuesdays he slept over at his father's.

"Ben!"

A child's love is selfish. A child's love is necessity. That gone, it either rekindles into admiration or lies to rest in a bed of memories, more or less comfortable, more or less relevant. My cruel memory always reminded me of my mistakes, of every time I'd hurt him without meaning to. But sometimes I did mean it; sometimes I wanted him to understand, gradually sucking that joyful spark from his eyes, gradually amounting a heaviness of dirt in his soul as I dug my grave in his heart. Maybe it was only my genes in him that I had come to recognise, but, either way, I was guilty; and being it a Tuesday, I wasn't about to start making up for anything.

"Ben!"

I wheeled myself down the hallway; no sign of him in his room. My fists squeezed the armrests; little shit had left without telling me. His father's voice bouncing within my walls, "I*s it time he moved in with me yet?*"—an infinite parade of little white worms gliding out of my peripheral vision, a dull blackness descending.

I knew my own darkness when I saw it, cruelly, slowly, sluggishly setting in. Setting in always but never set, so that I'd have time to fear it, feel it in my bare dim foyer of existence, hear it screech with rubber on the lino flooring as I turned and went. *I simply don't exist. I only exist when*

I hurt him. I am only pain—the ramp rattling loudly under my wheels as I rolled onto the driveway.

Despite the openness of the white sky, I remained far within the shadow of death's fist like a looming cave around me, a dormant wound killing me out of time. The brain scan had revealed a minor brain injury, but I had been unconscious for approximately three minutes, and nothing had ever been the same since, besides my obvious disability. Something had awoken. Something nobody else understood.

On I rolled, aware of my depleting battery, of time slowing with the leaves and branches as the rest of the world drifted out of scope. Wheels ran over an apple, a conker. But something ominous forced me to a stop.

"Ben?"

I turned an eternal turn, only to see an ominous nothing—my ominous house, the ominous air—hear a loud ominous coo from between the trees and the swaying, flapping. Hear the silence. See inside me the bright blue sky of a summer's day, feel it like a sheet of ice across a section of the brain.

I pressed my scalp with my palm, but I couldn't shake off the bag-of-peas-feeling, the sight of the wretched wood pigeon staring at me sideways with blind marble eyes. Not as it had happened when it happened a year or two before, or three—I lost sense of time sometimes—but perched on my windowsill, still and silent as the sky. A windowsill inside me. Even if I ignored it, even if I got distracted, the pigeon was always there.

***

"C'mon, Ben, just grab it!"

I'd tried poking the pigeon onto the Ronaldo shirt with the shovel, but the raw thing just kept flapping and falling, rolling, flapping, spitting like a sausage on the hot concrete. It always landed again on its feet, never dying, never not looking at me. Bright blue flies covered its featherless patches of chicken skin, a bloody glisten oozing from the scathed flesh as a cat licked its whiskers on the shed roof.

"Just grab it, Ben!"

There wasn't a chance on earth I'd have mustered the courage to grab the huge thing myself. Not that I didn't like animals, but I never had any pets. Poor Ben sobbed, angry with himself every time the thing bounced and he cowardly retracted.

I dragged him back into the house. I rang his father. But Ben insisted on checking on the damn thing every twenty minutes or so, still agonising, flapping, rolling in the backyard. I couldn't bear it anymore. His tears. Thomas said he wasn't "leaving work for a pigeon." The wildlife line never picked up.

I told Ben to hit it as hard as he could with a broomstick, but it rolled away from under each blow. Ben, my little Ben, purposefully hitting the slabs with the end of the stick, leaving a gap for it to escape. Once in the hideous situation, the only way out was to finish the job, make the ordeal worthwhile. I admit I shouted a lot, but Ben…he just didn't bring himself to do it.

Eventually his dad dropped by and took care of the thing's neck; wrapped it up in the Ronaldo shirt and twisted its head right off. They buried it together in a healing, bonding ceremony, Thomas shaking his head at me, wiping Ben's tears. Wiping Ben's tears with clean hands smelling of antibacterial.

"Mum told me to pick it up." "Mum said to hit it with a broomstick."

Next day the accident happened. A grey woman towered above me as I opened my eyes, regally positioned like a duchess in an old painting, gazing at me sideways in her stillness, amongst other bobbing faces. Someone was holding my hand as I called for Ben, the murmur of intelligible prayers bouncing on the other side of a glass barrier, a glass that stayed there through the weeks and months that followed. Separating me from the rest of the world.

Separating me still.

***

Something different swayed the trees. The village breathed emptiness; doors and windows swung open but not a soul stirred in or out of the vacant houses or shops, only the blowing curtains, the blinds hitting the window frames. Muffled playground noises flying overhead like distant kites, the distant motorway buzzing, as though the world was a memory. Like the empty village was flying, like the whole planet was this flat street and I rolling on the edge, to the sound of ghostly chirping wheels.

My bare arms bristled with awareness. Heightened senses on the nerve veins of every distant leaf rustling. Ben's small figure running around in the patch of green beyond the houses—an impossible sight from where I rolled, as I bypassed him forever on the endless road that never led to him.

Forest sounds grew loud and closer, my wheels reeling it in like an incoming treadmill belt—the concrete turning to grass and dirt. A forest glade. A sad light falling through the autumnal canopy, blessing a cluster of insects with beautiful timelessness.

I was standing on two legs, naked... I touched myself to make sure I wasn't dreaming, felt my younger chest heaving, the age I still saw myself as if I didn't look in a mirror, the adult I saw myself as during childhood. The 'finished me' I would grow into before the withering commenced and failure after failure succeeded one and the next. A past state-of-being, but the past that remains alive within you. The past that stays. A crossroad, in a forest glade.

The crisp sound of twigs breaking crept in from behind me. It penetrated my ears, one by one, like chicken bones reshaping me. Ben's football rolling right past me, carrying leaves and soil, prickling my back as the thudding of rubber soles ran through me and Ronaldo's number ten stretched the distance between us. Gliding down like a white butterfly, the ten alighted on the ball. Ben turned, brushing me obliviously as he ran back past me.

"Ben!"

My hands curled into fists, clenching hand-rests even if my chair wasn't there. I lifted my heel, but shackles of weight circled my ankles.

"Ben!"

The form of a woman, cloaked in shadow, emerged from between the trees. Her black boots trod from under the overreaching hem of her skirt, gradually solid like cloth and feather, but her face remained veiled by cloud so that I couldn't see her features—only a single defined pupil hovering in a blur of grey.

I forgot my shackles and fell on my back. Her sideways gaze nearing, towering above me as I futilely tried to drag myself away. A terrible beaked nose filtered through the fog then her iris, grey like sky as she peered through and revealed her unfathomable face. I cooed. I cooed in fear. I cooed dense gurgles, slow frog bubbles bobbing, never bursting. My brain rattling within my skull, my jaw cracking, my bones crushing in the wind of a ferocious glass spade missing me, never hitting me, but severing me from everything. Pain was a memory too.

She grasped my hands with bone and the smoothness of elderly palms. Three pink talon-fingers were wiggling impossibly at both sides of her cloak, yet she had me, pulled me to my feet with the grandmother hands as the worm-pink talons rose to clasp my chin. She shook my face lovingly, as though she couldn't resist the cuteness of a small child. Another child I'd let down.

A fog tunnel stretched as she trod backwards, allowing light to filter through the cloud. Beams of yellow lit up rainbow flowers and lime green grass shoots, exuding the bright fluff of dreams.

Deliverer of good or bad news? I didn't know. But she told me in her silence, with her sinister smile that *that* was my choice—fluff condensing into tiny tears, covering it all with dew and beautiful weight.

A stone over spilling me, I wept.

She turned, revealing her back to me. Patches of peeled skin glistened in the sunshine; sad feathers, semi-plucked out, hung from her shoulders like defeated arrows. With a brisk movement of the neck, she prompted me to follow her.

I followed her, submitted, will-less legs like wheels taking me down the pull of her magnetism. This was how I always went along, pulled by something stronger than me. Excuses. Twigs and dry leaves cracking, asphalt and grit and flattened beer cans. But my forehead hit the glass, palms stretched as I watched her standing in a different world. A takeaway sign. A pharmacy.

I gripped my armrests, but I found a spade. Painfully heavy I lifted it and thrust it against the glass, but really the spade pulled me, and she the spade. I trod on crushed glass until we found ourselves standing on a street, mute sirens flashing and spinning as we squeezed in through a crowd of onlookers.

There I was in the centre, spread on the tarmac. A sheet of glass slicing through my head. Her cold harsh finger seeking my hand, squeezing it as fondly as fear can comfort.

I looked at my broken body. The real 'finished me' lying there, the one at the other side of my windowsill, keeping me awake at night and startling me awake every morning, telling me to seize the day, telling me to love each one. Didn't I know how happy I was? Yes, I knew it. *Please… If I could have just one more chance.* Ben's small head sinking in the grey duchess's skirt as long claws ran through his hair.

I saw his eyes flooding. I saw them break like shattered glass, studding his heart with icicle rain, prickly needles like a morning star to both hurt and shield. I saw him slam the door. I saw him tell me *'I hate you.'* I saw him watch other mothers kicking a ball with their children, skiing down slopes, sliding down watery toboggans. I saw him cry on his father's knee. Thomas always said boys should be with their fathers.

A fog curtain sweeping my face with clarity, I surfaced from the woman's iris, back to the sound of robins chirping. A soothing forest shell like the mother Ben outgrew, as I stubbornly attempted to keep him in my tear-bubble, clinging to him selfishly. But haunting him with my pool of blood and red-stained clothes, a nightmare he could never bury, whether I lived or died.

I don't know who I'm giving my soul to. I don't nod nor shake my head, but she knows I've surrendered. Wings flap behind me, weakest ear bone struggling to lift the weight of my uselessness. But, perched as I am on her pink talon-fingers, she lifts me as far as her arm can stretch and throws me to the leaves above, memory weighing me uselessly down but, somehow, I stay off the ground, and I push and I flap and I soar; I soar for a moment and, next, a twig is sinking under my weight.

I look to the eyes in between the branches, mutely screaming their incarceration—that is why their eyes always looked so loud, I understood now, their terrible silence. My head bobbing, sinking into the nest of feathers of my chest as I confirm, this is as far as my wings were always going to take me, as high as I was ever going to fly. Perhaps he may swaddle me next time he buries me, he larger and I smaller, for in his garden I will remain.

***

A green line flattens in the vital signs monitor, a loud ringing in my ear.

I see a nurse's face looking at me sideways, Ben's eye narrowing as he lifts the slingshot and pulls the rubber, aiming to a startled pupil between the leaves. The rest of his world a surrounding fog of oblivion, for a moment.

SECRETS NEVER DIE

By J.W. Garrett

Jessica flipped through her calendar at work, noting all the appointments for the week, then scrolled to the monthly view. She drew a deep breath, shocked at her oversight. How could it sneak up on her?

Had it really been almost another year? She double-checked the dates. Yes—in three weeks it would be six years since her son's death.

Every year her husband's depression lasted for weeks. Preparing for his onslaught of emotions exhausted her. Maybe an evening out the night before; that might do it. Rehashing all the old feelings didn't help. Besides, Alex was five now and very sensitive to her parents' moods. Each year keeping her in the dark was more difficult than the last.

They always had the same argument. *What purpose would it serve to tell her now? He's dead. Nothing will bring Noah back.*

Her mind wandered as she packed her

briefcase with the few items she needed to take home. Images flashed in her head. Squeezing her eyes shut, she tried to free herself from the memory—*Mommy! Help! Mommy!* His scream echoed through her body, momentarily paralyzing her.

"Jess… Jess? Are you okay?"

The voice yanked her back to the present.

She blinked. "Yes. Fine, thanks."

"Good. You looked a little pale for a second. Have a great weekend."

"Yeah, you too, Tom."

The wind whipped her skirt between her legs as she made her way to the car, an involuntary shiver seizing her. As she closed the door and turned over the ignition, the fallen leaves spiralled through the air, and the clouds collided in dark, morose masses, matching her mood.

This time of year is the pits, so dreary and dark.

Thirty minutes later, the rain chasing her escape, the busy cityscape changed to a rural countryside. Rolling hills had replaced tall skyscrapers, and she prepared to turn onto the two-lane highway taking her to their country retreat. She parked beside her husband's car and hurried inside, the short trek drenching her clothing.

"There you are. I was wondering if you'd beat the storm."

"No. Of course not."

Her husband looked her over from head to toe and smiled. "You do look a little like a drowned rat."

"That was positively rude, Jason, and I'm not in the mood. I'm dripping wet."

"Well, I can redeem myself," he said, biting back laughter. "Voilà, dinner is started. It'll be ready in thirty minutes. Your adorable daughter is playing in the barn as we speak, churning up mud on her bike. And a glass of wine awaits you on the counter."

She peered over his shoulder. "Ah, just what I need." She attempted to manoeuvre past him, but he blocked her path. "Now what?" she asked, wanting the wine more than she cared to admit.

"It's going to cost you. I'd say the price is…a shirt and skirt. Sound fair to you?" he asked, raising his eyebrows.

"What about your daughter in that creepy old barn?"

He cocked his head to the side. "Take a look, you can see her from here—she's having a blast."

"It appears you have an answer for everything," she said, rolling her eyes.

"Except the question on the table. Shirt and skirt," he announced, swirling the wine in invitation.

She shrugged. "Okay, you win. But only because I'm making a puddle where I stand, and I need to take them off anyway." She wiggled out of the wet skirt and let it fall to the floor. "Now hand over the wine."

"Nope. That wasn't the deal. The shirt too."

"Maybe I'm renegotiating."

A wicked grin slid to his face. "That could possibly be arranged. Follow me."

She turned the corner into the family room where a fire crackled in the fireplace.

"*Mmm.* You've been busy. I'd call this entrapment."

He set the glass on the side table, and as she reached for it, he loosened the buttons of her shirt and pulled the damp clothing off her shoulders.

Jess took two gulps of wine. Two more large swallows later, the anxiety from earlier dissipating, she allowed herself to be led to the couch.

"You have exactly five minutes. Then I'm headed for the shower," she warned.

He chuckled. "This is going to take longer than that." Jess opened her mouth in protest, and he silenced her with a kiss. "No more talk," he murmured. "Our daughter could be back any minute. Remember?"

"But—"

"*Shhh*."

***

"That was—"

"Mommy…"

"Athletic."

A grin played at the corner of his mouth as he reached for his clothes.

The front door slammed.

"Your daughter has perfect timing, just like her mother," he said with a wink, pulling on his pants and grabbing his shirt.

"Entertain her while I take a shower

and finish my wine. Would you?" she asked, following her trail of clothing and retreating to the bathroom.

Twenty minutes later a soft knock sounded on the bathroom door. "Daddy said dinner's ready. Come eat, Mommy."

"Be right there, sweetheart."

Jessica dressed and strolled to the kitchen minutes later. The mood in the room had shifted, charged with a completely different type of energy than earlier this evening, threading through the space, chilling her skin. Worry creased her husband's forehead as he served the food. Her gaze darted from her husband wound tight, to her daughter, the picture of innocence.

What is it? she mouthed, tuning in to

Alex's excited conversation.

"We had fun playing outside, Daddy. Why are you mad?"

"We? Someone was playing with you?" Jess asked. "Daddy didn't tell me that we had company," she added, glaring at her husband.

"Daddy didn't know," Jason said with a huff. "What did you do out there?"

"What was his name?" Jess asked.

"He was teaching me to ride a two-wheeler—a real bike! And I think he said his name was Noah."

Jessica's glass slid from her fingers, shattering as it hit the tile floor. Jason faced his wife, colour leaching from his face.

"Are you sure his name was Noah?" Jason asked, bending to Alex's level and grabbing one of her arms.

"Yes, Daddy. Why are you acting so funny, and why are your fingers sweaty?" she asked, squirming free.

"Where is he now?" he asked.

"Noah said he'd wait for me, and we'd play again tomorrow."

"He's still here?"

"I dunno, Daddy."

Jason turned to Jess, already cleaning up the broken glass. "Stay with her. I'm going to check out the barn."

Grabbing a flashlight, he stormed from the kitchen, rattling the door as he slammed it shut.

"Sit still while I clean up the glass."

Her heart thumped loudly, pounding a rhythm in her chest while she waited for her husband to return. Fighting her rising panic, she paced the cold tile floor. Still, the minutes dragged as they ticked idly by. Her eyes focused in quick succession, alternating from the light under the barn door in the distance, to the clock in the kitchen. *Six minutes…* The light flickered off inside the barn, and her gaze tracked the path as her husband progressed toward the house.

"Well?" she gasped when he shut the door behind him, beads of sweat dotting her forehead. "Was anyone out there?"

"No. No one. But I could see two sets of footprints in the mud. One set looked like boots, and the other set matched the shoes Alex was wearing," he said, motioning to the muddy pair parked by the door. He lowered his voice to a whisper. "We should eat dinner and let the rest of this conversation wait until morning. We need more information, but I don't want to scare her."

***

Jess coaxed her daughter into the bathtub. "Ugh…" Waiting until morning for answers would not do... The water coloured, turning a dull brown as the mud on Alex's body washed away. Her daughter filled a toy bucket with water, splashed it on herself, then erupted into giggles. *Clearly the playtime in the barn wasn't upsetting her.*

"Alex, tell me more about Noah, from

the barn. What did he look like?"

Alex stopped splashing and glanced at her mother. "Whadda you mean, Mommy?"

"Well, what was he wearing? What colour was his hair? And anything else you can remember."

Alex squealed. "Is this a game? He's a *boy*. And his hair is black. And he sang a song about sheep."

Jess drew a deep breath, then coughed loudly, trying to cover her response. *How could it be? It's not possible*. She rushed her daughter through the remainder of her bath.

"Did I win, Mommy?"

"Yes, sure, Alex."

"What did I win, Mommy?"

An early trip to bed. "Let's go. Out of the tub. Time for lights out."

Jess hurried her daughter through her bedtime rituals, eager to be alone with her thoughts.

"Good night, dear," Jess said, her finger poised on the light switch. "Have a good sleep."

"Mommy, are you mad at me?"

"No, Alex. Mommy's just tired. I'll see you in the morning."

Jess flipped the switch and softly closed the door. Padding to the guest room, she held her breath, paused, her hand lingering on the doorknob a few seconds before opening the door and ducking inside. She blinked, then froze seeing the room as it had been years ago, when her son had occupied this space.

No, no, no! Stop this. It's silly. Squeezing her eyes tight against the vision, she shook her head. *It's not real...* Slowly lifting her eyelids, she heaved a deep sigh, the vision gone. Scurrying through the doorway she rushed to her own bedroom.

I have to let this nonsense go.

"Jason, are you asleep?" she asked, crawling under the covers.

"Yes."

She stared at his back, pulled down the covers, and drew him closer. His shoulder shrugged away her hand.

"Jason, we need to talk."

He turned abruptly and sat up, balancing on his forearm. "What's there to say? Our daughter is spending time playing with our dead son—the brother she never knew. Everything's perfect."

"Jason, calm down. We don't have to argue." Jess reached for him and leaned in for a kiss.

"No," he said, pulling away from her. "You want to talk? Let's talk," he said, his voice coming out in a streaming hiss. "I find myself envious of my daughter because I'd give anything to talk to my son again. To tell him how much I love him. To tell him I'm sorry I wasn't there for him…"

Even in the semidarkness, Jess could see the flash of anger in her husband's eyes as she met his stoic stare.

"To get some answers. Your amnesia at the point of his death left many unanswered questions. What do *you* want to know? Huh?" He swung his legs over the side of the bed and grabbed his robe. "I would think those unanswered questions would bother you. But it seems I'm the only one wrecked here."

And so it had begun.

"In order to move forward, I let this go years ago," she replied. "But you never did. You know this, yet we struggle through this same battle every year dredging up the pain. It's pointless."

He flashed her a glare, grief etched into the hard lines of his face. Defusing the situation had gone to shit.

"Maybe I can't wrap up my feelings in a neat little package and put it on a shelf and forget it, like you can." He ran his fingers through his hair. "I'm not sure what's going on, but I'm going to spend tomorrow getting some answers." He rose, grabbed his pillow, and headed for the bedroom door.

"Where are you going?"

"To the couch. I won't fall asleep anytime soon, and I wouldn't want to keep you awake."

His sarcastic tone wasn't lost on her, but she wouldn't chase him. She reclined on her pillow and scooted deeper under the covers.

What a mess.

***

Jessica startled awake. *What was that?* She glanced at the clock. *God, 3:00 a.m.*

Why am I awake? She peered into the darkness, her senses on edge. *There it is again...* She listened, struggling to decipher the words. *Sounds like humming.*

Pulling on her robe, Jessica plodded down the hall, searching for the source of the noise. *It must be Alex.* Her daughter's bedroom door stood ajar; Jess nudged through the space and turned on the light. No Alex…

The humming started again. *It can't be.* The childlike voice singing sent a shiver down her spine. He used to ask her to sing it repeatedly. Every night.

She followed the melody and hesitated in front of the guest room door. The voice came out muffled, portions fading in and out, but she knew it well.

Bah, bah…

Jess pushed through the guest room door to find her daughter's back facing her. Something was in her hand. "Stop that, Alex. Why are you out of bed?"

The singing came to a halt, and Alex spun to face her. The streetlight flooded the room, bringing an eerie unnatural highlight to her daughter's expression. Jess's blood went cold. The way she held her mouth, scrutinized Jess with her steely gaze…

"Alex?"

"I needed to visit my sheep."

Jess took a step backward, shook her head. *This can't be.* The voice was… *Noah's.* "Where did you get that, Alex?"

"In my drawer. It took me some time to find it," she said, hugging the sheep closer. "Why did you hide it?"

"Come on. Put that down. Back to bed. You're sleepwalking. Let's go, Alex."

"Mommy, why do you keep calling me Alex? I'm Noah. Call me *Noah*."

Jess stumbled as she reached for the door, her mouth moving but no words coming out. *Noah? How... Why?*

"I, I...must be dreaming."

Everything was off with her. The way her head cocked to the left, the deep sadness hanging in her eyes, her tone of voice. The silent stillness of the room engulfed Jess as her gaze focused on the child living, yet dead; she couldn't turn away. *How could it be?*

Alex's rag doll lay on the floor. *Stupid doll. It doesn't do anything, just stuffing and cloth. And she loves the thing*. Efforts over the years to replace it with better, more elaborate dolls had failed. Now, there it was, sprawled on the floor, donning the same lifeless expression throughout all its days. Jess sidestepped to pick it up.

"Alex, come here. I've got Silvie. Drop the sheep, and let's go back to bed. Come on."

She stood up defiantly. "I told you. I'm Noah!"

Jess instinctively took a step forward and raised her hand to slap her daughter, dropping the rag doll in the process. Grabbing her mother's wrist mid-air as it came down, Alex held tight. Jess twisted and pulled. "Alex, let go." Fear bubbled up in the pit of her stomach as she stifled a sob.

"Don't hurt my sister like you hurt me. Why do you want to hurt her?"

"Alex, honey," Jess managed to say through her tears. "I'm trying to wake you. You're asleep. Let go of my arm please, and let's get you back to bed."

A grin settled on her daughter's face. One Jess hadn't seen in almost six years, and her heart beat faster, echoing loudly in her ears.

"Alex is with *me* now, and she wants to play!" Her daughter laughed heartily and collected Silvie from where she had fallen, momentarily forgotten. Then Alex dashed from the room.

Stunned, Jess stood stuck in place. She stared down the empty hallway where her daughter had just fled, willing her bare feet to move. A loud clap of thunder blasted outside, jolting her back to reality. Then shuddering out a breath, she put one foot in front of the other and followed her daughter. Ahead, the front door opened, swayed in the wind, and Jess picked up the pace, running now to find Alex.

Passing her sleeping husband on the couch, she debated whether to wake him for a split second. No, she'd handle this on her own. He couldn't hear the things Alex was saying—not now, not ever.

Outside, steady driving rain fell in sheets, pelting her face. Laughter rang out in the distance. Dread threatened to immobilize her as the light flickered on in the barn.

Mud gathered around her feet and

seeped between her toes, making sucking noises with each slippery step forward. Sliding along the walkway, she edged closer to the barn. A stream of light bathed a short path from underneath the barn door. Giving the door a shove, it swung open with a loud squeak. Grateful to be out of the deluge for the moment, she squeezed inside.

Jess drew her arms around herself, shivering as she eyed the place. Muffled squeals seemed to come from everywhere. She glanced to opposite sides of the room, tracking the noise, clearly hearing two sets of voices.

"Alex, come out now. It's not time to play. It's time for bed." Jess cinched her drenched mud-soaked robe tighter and moved to the centre of the barn, checking side to side so she wouldn't be startled if Alex jumped out at her. "Where are you?" she asked, spinning in circles, desperation creeping into her voice.

"Here I am. Come and get me," she said, giggling, scaling the wooden steps to the barn's second floor. Silvie's head bobbed up and down from her position clutched tightly in the crook of Alex's arm as she climbed higher and higher, mocking Jess down below.

Where did Alex drop the sheep? She couldn't have her husband finding that old thing. The steps to the upper level groaned and creaked under her weight. Her robe caught on a nail, and she ripped it free, almost losing her balance in the process.

Grasping both sides of the stairs, she emerged into the loft; short of breath and gasping for air, she called again to her daughter.

"Alex," she yelled, her tone icy and shrill. "Enough is enough."

"Here I am, Mommy," she announced popping out from the shadows. "And here is Noah."

Both walked toward her, the boy, reunited with the sheep, and her daughter, clinging to Silvie in a death grip.

Jess reached out a steadying hand, but with no wall close by, she stumbled and fell instead. "Noah? But Noah's dead," she whispered, crawling backward.

"I'm right here, Mommy. You can see me," he said, stretching his arms wide in confirmation.

"No, no, no… You're not real. You're dead! Go away, and leave us alone."

"Tell her, Mommy," he said, inching closer. "Tell Alex what you did to me. How you left me to die."

"What? I didn't do that. That's not true." Uncontrollable sobs wracked her body as she scooted toward the wall.

"You shouldn't lie, Mommy. You should tell the truth. I came to be with my sister. Now that I know her, I'm never leaving. *You* don't deserve her. Me and Alex, we'll be together always."

Jess watched them, their hands clasped together, as they ambled slowly toward her.

"Why didn't you tell me that I had a brother?" Alex asked, drawing closer still.

Jess reached out for her daughter, her chest heaving as she tried to catch her breath. "I wanted to, Alex. Really, I did."

Noah shook his head. "You did bad things, Mommy. But no more."

Jess clawed to a stand and, with small steps, balanced along the upper floor. "Noah, it was an ac-ac-ac…accident."

Her son's gaze bore through her. "No more lies."

Alex loosened her grip, then released Noah's hand and charged her mother. Jess's jaw dropped as her maniacal child unleashed upon her. Frantically, she groped for something to grab, but flailing her arms, she found only air. With a shriek reverberating throughout the barn, Alex hit her head-on, her daughter's arms encircling her mother's waist, tipping the balance between life and death. Hurtling to the ground below, they landed in a clash of flesh and bone.

***

Jason sat upright, immediately awake at the sound of his wife's scream. He rushed outside, then into the barn, and circled the pair of bodies sprawled at unnatural angles on the floor. Blood flowed from gaping head wounds in both of them. He fell to his knees as he slid his daughter into his lap. Supported by his arms, the lifeless body bounced back and forth aimlessly to a silent rhythm.

He buried his face into his daughter's

hair as he rocked. "Not again, not again. I should have burned this damn barn down."

"Papa?"

Jason lifted his head and met his son's gaze. His mouth fell open. He tenderly laid down his daughter, pausing to move a stray strand of hair from her face, then turned to face Noah, perched on the second floor of the barn.

"Noah? Am I dreaming? Is it really you?"

"It'll be okay. You'll see," he said, descending to the first floor and into his father's arms.

A tingling sensation filled Jason as the boy's body pressed against his own. After examining every inch of his son, as if confirming his validity, Jason hugged him close again.

"I didn't believe Alex," Jason said, inhaling deeply, remembering his son's scent. A deep sigh rippled through his chest, the current tragedy mingling with the memory of the older one, almost six years ago.

Noah disengaged from the embrace. "It's me, Papa…and Alex."

Jason studied the boy in front of him, the only one who had ever called him Papa. *It has to be him.* Jason peered into the distance at the back of the barn, blinking when she bounced into view. He collapsed backward, his gaze snapping toward the two dead bodies for affirmation.

"Alex? How can it be? I don't understand," he said, tears falling down his cheeks accompanying a fresh wave of grief.

"Don't worry, Daddy. It was hard for me at first too. Noah explained it to me, and he will for you also. Anytime you want to see us, just come out to the barn. We'll always be here. We'll never leave you." Alex cuddled her rag doll close.

Silvie's button eyes blinked, and the thread-sewn mouth turned upward, forming a grin.

SOMETHING TO FALL BACK ON

By Beth W. Patterson

The tiniest clink of metal on metal yanks me from a sound sleep. My clock reads 3:58 AM. Someone is trying to tiptoe around my bed. I can barely make out a female silhouette and I catch a whiff of flowers. I don't recall having had two women, at least not tonight. But it's always a possibility, as I think I look pretty good for a man of fifty.

Susie is still asleep next to me, fresh-faced and perfect as a spun-sugar doll. She always did fall asleep first at my daughter Amelia's slumber parties, tempting the other girls to punk her quite a bit. We're both pretty fortunate now; lucky for her because no one will mess with her while she's in my bed, and lucky for me because the consenting age in West Virginia is sixteen. So if this intruder is from child protection, I haven't done anything wrong. I'd even told all the parents last night— including Amelia's mom—that I'd drive both Susie and Amelia to school, and nobody batted an eye.

But the person in the bedroom looks familiar. She could almost pass for . . .

"Vera!" I blurt out, stifling myself mid-word into a whisper. "What are you doing here?"

My co-worker has a penchant for practical jokes, but she's never entered my house unbidden before. She's moderately attractive, even if she's only nine years my junior. "Hey, Dan. I've got something funny to tell you!"

I start snickering right away, and I don't even know why. Vera and I always cut up when we're working together at Honey Bug Appliance Repairs, so maybe I just associate her with humour. She also comes in handy when I've had a few beers after hours and I can't find anyone better to fuck. "Well, what is it?" I finally ask her.

"Check this shit out, Dan! I'm dead!"

"What?" Now I'm really laughing. "What sort of prank are you up to?"

"No, really!" she insists, pulling her flannel shirt more tightly around herself. "Go on . . . touch me anywhere!"

Instinctively I want to grab her breast, but I use my better judgment in case Susie should wake, so I reach for Vera's cheek. My hand passes right through, only hitting frigid air like a hologram in a freezer.

"Come on," I snort, "How are you pulling this off? Where are you? This is an awesome effect . . ." My eyes scan the room for some sort of projector, but the longer I chat, the less certain I am that it's one of her tricks.

She smiles that familiar lopsided grin, her long copper curls falling over her eyes. "No, it's real," she sighs. "Your most reliable backup plan—that would be me— is no more. I was repairing a cappuccino machine at a restaurant, and those idiots had forgotten to unplug it and dump the water out of it first. Electrical shock is a helluva way to go."

I don't know which is worse: that Vera might really be dead or that she just called me out for using her body as a last resort lay. After all, she wanted it as badly as I did, and I never told her that I loved her back.

I have to change the subject fast. "So,

uh . . . what's being dead like? I thought you were supposed to be in heaven. Isn't that why Christ died for us?" Maybe if I start talking about Adonai and sin and forgiveness, she'll go away.

"It's so *funny!*" She bursts into that wheezing laugh I know so well. "All the things people stress out about—taxes, beauty, wealth, fame—it doesn't matter in the end! You living should see yourselves, all running about like chickens with their heads cut off.

"And then there are other forces about, like faery mischief. Now that I'm a spirit, I can see the cause of all the things you find so annoying: WiFi suddenly going out, car tires mysteriously going flat, water pipes bursting . . . all the work of faeries!"

I don't want to believe her, but I've already put my hand on a dead person's cheek, so what have I got to lose? "Well, uh, how do I protect myself from them?"

"With iron, silly!" she chortles. "It's the one thing that repels them. Get yourself a good wrought iron fence like they make in New Orleans and put it around your house. They say good fences make good neighbours, and your pad will look pretty classy. The iron will ward off curses, help you locate misplaced items, and even conceal evidence from concerned parents…"

"Hmmm." I try to appear unconvinced, but I guess holding a conversation with a ghost is a dead giveaway.

"Here's the secret," she continues. "The fences have to have spikes along the top. Some of the more malevolent spirits drag their hair, their chains, or even their guts behind them as they fly through the air, so if you have spikes the fey get snagged on them and can't go near your house."

An agitated murmur next to me makes me jump. I don't want to wake up little Susie. My new conquest stirs, sighs, and purrs like a kitten before falling back into a deep slumber. When I look back up, Vera is gone.

***

My weird dream bothers me all

morning. I manage to shake it off after my second cup of coffee, but when I arrive at Honey Bug, everyone is noticeably upset. Before I can open my mouth, my boss Patrick breaks the news to me about Vera's passing: death by electrocution. He mistakes the expression on my face for shock, but I'm just horrified that her spectral visit was real.

Later that day, I'm cranky because I haven't slept much, I have twice as much work to do without Vera there, and all anyone can talk about is that stupid bitch who got herself shocked. At one point, Patrick claps a hand on my back, and I jump out of my skin before rounding on him. On any other day this outburst could have gotten me fired, but that dumbass thinks I'm just bereaved and lets me take the rest of the day off.

At home, I look online and find some ready-made wrought iron panels with spears across the top. I can almost feel Vera's gaze over my shoulder, as if she's guiding my hand while I scroll through the choices. I land on an opulent design of spirals, ivy leaves, and wicked-looking spears along the top. Nearly of its own volition, my hand clicks "buy" before I can stop myself. The panels are more than I can afford, so Amelia will just have to work a second job when she gets to college.

This fence is far more important.

***

It's been three weeks since I ordered the damned iron works. Plus each night since the electrocution Vera has paid me a visit, throwing my sleep cycle out of whack. So by the time the deliveryman arrives, I'm tired, stressed, and irritable with everyone. No one else in the neighbourhood has ever bothered with fences, so passers-by regard me with suspicion as I try to install it.

Nothing motivates raising a fence like rage. Susie and I had a fight earlier today. She wants to go to prom with a boy in her class, but I consider her to be mine and mine alone. I pretend that I'm teaching her a lesson as I dig postholes in the ground with my auger drill, the massive corkscrew spattering flecks of tender earth into the air.

I'm almost a danger to myself with the hacksaw, but force myself to calm down and focus. I don't want to spend all day redoing this. If the neighbours are suddenly afraid of me, so much the better.

But as the sun sets and my frustrations are somewhat vented, my mood eases. The fence looks pretty good, its ornate rococo turning my otherwise shabby little house into a gothic estate. It's especially striking at night, part of it nearly invisible in the shadows and part of it shining in the moonlight.

"Go Dan! You did it! You've not only increased your property value, but now you're nice and safe from supernatural mischief!" I look up to see Vera crouched like a cat on the roof. The top two buttons of her shirt are open, practically inviting me to squeeze her tits. Maybe it's the fact that death makes a person ageless, but she looks even younger than Susie now. It would certainly show that little princess a thing or two if I made it with a chick who looks younger and hotter than her, even a dead person.

"Can you see the faeries?" she calls out. "The imps and goblins are fleeing by the dozens from your property line!"

"No way!" I shout back.

"Come on, get up on the roof with me!" she insists. "I'll let you see them through my vision. Bring your eyes near mine."

I run for the ladder by my tool shed and scramble up to meet her. Vera looks pale and perfect, her smile exceptionally beguiling as I draw nearer. I lean in until my face is nearly touching hers.

With a guttural scream, the dead woman lunges at me. Her eyes become two hollow black pits, her face a fanged skull. Scared shitless, my entire body freezes as she reaches for my face with a bony hand. This time I instinctively jump backward, losing my balance on the slanted roof. I barely have time to process what's happening in the split second between falling and landing heavily onto the spikes of my fence with a sound of wet, meaty tearing. My world explodes in a red haze of pain. I grab at the warm, slick spires protruding through my chest and abdomen.

Vera, sweet-faced and pretty once

more, floats down to meet my gaze. "You always did need something to fall back on, didn't you?" she purrs.

I convulsively jerk around like a speared fish. My body isn't going anywhere. The more I panic, the more the torture increases.

"Careful! If you pull yourself off of that fence, you'll just bleed to death!" she cheerfully informs me. My body weight just drags the spires deeper, the ornate fence grating against my ribs and spine. I feel something inside me give way, part of the iron point punctures a lung, and I gasp for breath only to inhale my own blood.

I can't control the low groans tearing from my throat. I fill my mind with God and Jesus and beg them to help me either pass out from the agony or just die.

The last thing I hear before everything goes black is Vera cackling, "Aren't you a little bit old to be believing in faeries?"

STANDING STONES

By David Bowmore

He watched the small boat chug back to the mainland and the security of civilisation. It had been his agent's idea; a chance to live on a deserted island for a month, with little modern convenience where he could draw to his heart's content. As a marketing ploy, it was bound to garner interest.

For the self-enforced sabbatical, he had chosen Creigearan Creige, the largest of a group of three land masses to the west of Scotland and north of Ireland. It had the added appeal of getting him out of the city and away from its festival-goers and tourists. Edinburgh during the summer was hot and overcrowded. He had camping gear and provisions, his canvases and oils, sketch pads and pencils and a handful of mystery paperbacks. Nothing, however, in the form of modern tech. What would be the point? The island was devoid of electricity.

He made his way towards higher ground and found a stone circle consisting of thirteen boulders. Unlucky for some, but clearly not for the ancients who had once brought their dead here.

He positioned his tent beyond the stones in subsurface furrows and lanes, the foundations of habitat that had been excavated some thirty years previously. Sitting six feet below ground level, it gave good protection from the Atlantic winds. After gathering kindling and fallen branches, he lit his fire, ate a self-heating ration of mystery mince, and settled down for the night.

By day, he wandered the island. There really wasn't much to it. Stone circles, the odd standing stone, labyrinthine corridors, semi revealed dwellings, cliffs, a beach of sorts, and a copse of woodland. He explored, sketched the stones, daubed on his canvases. The sunny and glorious days were a complete contrast to the nights.

It was before dawn on his third night when he was first woken by the sound of distant noises, squealing or howling. *Howling?* The island was almost devoid of life, and the small forest was home to nothing larger than rodents. But wolves? Britain had not had wolves for hundreds of years. He stoked the fire and splashed water in his face. Then, silence. *Must have been the wind.*

For several nights, he was woken just before dawn by the far-off sound of a company of wolves. He set his watch alarm earlier to avoid the howling in his dreams. When he was fed, washed, and ready for the day, he was pleased to have heard nothing remotely wolfish. This became his new ritual and had the added satisfaction of giving his work a new spiritual perspective, thanks to the morning light.

Halfway through his adventure, and not long after having turned in for the night, he has woken by scratching and snuffling somewhere above him at ground level. It sounded like a large animal pawing at the ground. Then he heard an aggressive snapping snarl followed by a whimper, one beast telling another to back off. Shaking, he tried to silence the chattering of his teeth.

What do I do?

Be brave, he heard his mother say.

He sprinted from his lair, up the steps, yelling at the top of his lungs, "Aarghhh, come on ye furry bastards. Arhhhhh.”

His battle cry died as he realised he was alone, but paw tracks and claw marks in the soft soil would soon be revealed in the light of the early morning sun.

He couldn't sleep; he wouldn't sleep. Not at night. During the day, he grabbed the odd hour, but at night, he was on guard. He fancied he saw movement on the edge of the small woodland, but he wasn't going to put himself in danger by going to investigate. It was a ridiculous notion; the small island couldn't possibly support a pack of wolves. What would they live on? Yet, at night, the sounds of the pack still surrounded him and he continued to see movement in the distant shadows.

Deprived of sleep, aware of the smell of

his unwashed body, and with the month's supply of rations exhausted, he bitterly regretted the foolhardy idea of coming to a deserted island. He would gladly put up with an overcrowded Edinburgh Castle over this desperate hole any day of the week. Only a few days to go before the boat returned.

Sitting in his camp chair, his fire dwindling, his head nodding, he was brought to by a sharp bark beyond the edge of the wood, followed by another and another. The animal noises combined and lengthened into strange high-pitched howls from the copse of trees up ahead.

He stood, his legs shaking uncontrollably, and strained to see the activity at the edge of the wood some five hundred metres away, illuminated only by the silver glow of the moon. Then, sudden movement, so fast and elegant he forgot his fear and wished he had a camera to capture the three graceful shapes converging in the distance.

Taking a blind step backwards, he crashed into the pit of the ancient house. Something snapped in his shoulder; the pain was immense. Grasping at it with his good hand, he felt the sharp edge of bone protruding through flesh.

A new wave of nausea passed over him as an animal landed in front of him. The wolf, if indeed it was a wolf, was standing like a man on its hind legs at well over eight feet tall. The stench of rotten meat turned his stomach for a third time. His attempt to shuffle away from the creature was halted by a large paw pushing down on his chest. Sharp claws began to pierce his skin as the beast exerted pressure. The rat-like eyes of the monster reflected the full moon, and its mouth curled in a wicked grin to reveal yellow incisors dripping with drool. Its bald tail flicked and twitched as the pointed head lowered.

A few days later, the small boat returned to collect the castaway. The crew found nothing living on the island larger than a rodent.

First published in *Dastaan Magazine*, 2018

SUPPLY RUN

By Chris Bannor

You should never have left her.

Mo jerked awake quickly. She could still hear the voice in her ear, but no one was there. She stared into the empty sleeping compartment around her, heart racing, but she was alone. She let out a shuttered breath before she walked out of the narrow room. She left the enclosed area to go to the main cabin just to make a quick check. It was just an excuse to get away from her solitude.

When she sat down at the monitor she went through a diagnostic on the ship as well. The readings were all normal as she'd expected, but the act of checking calmed her. When she finished, she felt less jumpy. It was almost time for breakfast anyway, so she got dressed and started her day with a small meal. She ate in silence, her eyes staring out of the window and back towards the planet where Angelica waited for her.

You promised to stay by her side.

She flinched away as a woman appeared over her shoulder in the window's reflection. She jerked around, but there was no one there.

"I will not go crazy on a stupid supply run," she said with a shake of her head. Another specialist was supposed to be with her on the trip, but an injury had laid him up and a poor weather forecast made them decide to continue the supply run with just the captain.

"Angelica, baby, I am never watching horror movies with you again. I don't care what you promise in return." She smirked at the reminder of her wife's love of horror movies, and her ability to make Mo sit through things she would never in a million years pick out herself.

"And no more ghost stories about haunted jewelry and what your Great Aunt swore she saw either. I don't care who did what to whom in your family tree. No more."

Her vision was suddenly filled by an evening sky horrifyingly lit with fire, tall trees and bloody ropes, the stench of death in her nostrils and terror in her heart.

She jumped up and ran into the wall, tripping over her seat, and knocking herself to the ground as she did. When she opened her eyes, she was on the ship. There was nothing there but her and her imagination. She swallowed against the lump in her throat and slowly moved back to the pilot's seat. She pulled the cameo necklace out from under her uniform shirt and ran her fingers lightly over it. Angelica had given it to her right before departure; a good luck charm she'd said.

She turned on the communication array, but interference made it impossible to contact Mission Control. She'd wanted to talk to one of the counsellors they kept waiting in the wings just in case, but it didn't look like that was going to happen. Instead, she sent a message that would transmit as soon as they were through the obstruction.

"Mission Control, this is Captain Maureen Taylor. I have detected no signs of chemical or radiation leaks, but I have concerns about the equipment readings. I have begun to hallucinate voices and places that I have never been. I haven't slept well the last two nights. I'm jumping at air and…" She sighed. "It's only two days into the mission, and I already need a vacation.

"I have two more days until I reach the colony where I will report to their medical staff for evaluation. I will continue to send updates until the interference clears up, and I can speak with you directly. Captain Taylor, out." She turned off the equipment and sat back.

"Two more days, a week on the colony, and then a quick return, weather permitting. I'll be home soon, Angelica." She kissed the cameo and began to tuck the necklace away under her uniform. "See me back to my wife, alright?"

"I just gotta keep busy. Focus on the

mission," she told herself.

She had work to do, and so far, that was the only thing that seemed to settle her ever-growing nerves. She startled over every noise in the shuttle and she couldn't seem to calm her hyperactive responses. As she leaned over to reach her tablet, the white table blurred before her eyes and turned into a grave slab.

She jumped out of her chair and spun away from the vision, afraid to turn back. When she looked out the window to space though, she was being watched by dark eyes and terrifying accusations.

"Please, leave me alone," she begged. She scrambled into the sleeping compartment and pushed her back against the wall, curling up into the bed as if that could protect her. "Stop following me!" she screamed as she covered her head with her hands.

She could hear the sharp slap of a palm on the slick floor though, followed by the slide of something large being dragged through the shuttle. She whimpered and gripped her wife's cameo tighter as if it could hold off the spirits that haunted her.

She shrieked as she felt a hand grab onto her leg, but she refused to open her eyes and believe in this hallucination. She sobbed into her hands, heart racing, but she still clung to the logic that said this couldn't be happening.

The hand used her ankle to pull itself upright on the bed with her, and Mo pushed it away without success. "Get off!" she yelled.

You shouldn't have left her.

"I'm going back to her. I'm returning home. Leave me alone," she cried. "I didn't leave her!"

You left her alone. You will never return home.

A wordless, guttural sound escaped her lips but when she opened her eyes she was alone again. She fumbled out of the bed and tripped her way back to the cargo bay. She needed someplace open, someplace that didn't feel so much like a coffin.

The cold sucked at her skin, and she wondered at the sudden drop in temperature, but there were no alarms sounding. She looked through the window, fearful of seeing another strange face, but only the cargo hold lay beyond.

She took a deep breath and opened the door.

Lying on the floor of the bay just out of view of the window was a female body. She gasped as she moved closer, but stopped, terrified of what ghost would haunt her this time. After a few moments, she saw blood staining the woman's dark brown hair. It had caked and dried over the profile, making her unrecognizable from where she lay.

Fear made Mo weak, but now action called, and blood rushed in her veins again. She dropped to the woman's side and felt for a pulse. There was nothing. Her body was cold and rigor mortis had already left. She looked around the room and saw that next to her was a patch in the wall. An emergency job. Something had struck the bay and caused a hole. Had she been hit too? When could this have happened? How? Mo was alone on the ship.

Why don't you look at her face?

Mo closed her eyes and felt the tears building behind her eyelids. "Stop this! I didn't leave her!"

Why don't you look at her face?

"I didn't leave her!"

Look at her face! the voice wailed.

"No, I… I'm going home to her. I'm going home." She pulled the body away from the floor and sobbed. "I'm going home. I promised. I'm going home."

That's what we all said, and we died, one by one until the only thing left of our promises was a cameo, passed down, tormenting the souls of liars for hereafter.

Mo screamed, but there was no one to hear. She had died alone, patching a hole in the cargo bay.

#

After an emergency dock, people rushed aboard and found her lifeless body on the floor. She was called a hero for making the run that saved hundreds of lives.

Angelica Taylor received medals and awards to celebrate her wife's bravery. The only personal possession she'd had with her on the supply run was a cameo she wore around her neck. Angelica slipped the cameo on over her head, never knowing Mo followed the cameo home.

THE BOY

By Stephen Herczeg

"Don't know why they ignore me," thought the boy. "Must be my costume."

He picked another chocolate bar out of his bucket and unwrapped it. Lifting the sheet, he moved the chocolate up to his mouth and munched down.

"A ghost," he thought. "The best I could come up with was a ghost."

His mother had sacrificed the sheet and helped him cut holes for the eyes. When he'd told his friends about his costume they politely declined to go trick or treating with him. His mother found him crying on his bed. When he explained, she suggested that she could walk around with him. That horrified him more than not going with his friends. In the end his mother agreed to let him go off on his own, though he did notice the look of worry on her face as he walked away. Her last words were that she would meet him out front of the last house on the left on Elm Street at seven o'clock. That left him an hour to comb the suburban streets for those willing to part with candy in return for no tricks being played.

All went well. He peered down at the stash sitting in his little pumpkin-shaped bucket. It was full to the brim with chocolate bars, individually wrapped candy and other assorted sweet treats.

He finished the chocolate and unwrapped another. He figured he could get through several before his mother arrived. He'd tell her he only had a couple. He tossed the wrapper and fed the bar up under the sheet.

The sound of voices to his right grabbed his attention. He saw a small group of trick-or-treaters approaching. There were a couple of superheroes, a storm trooper, and a giggly pink witch. A father walked with them, holding the little witch's hand as they crossed the street towards him.

The entire group ignored the boy, and the little girl peered up the garden path leading to the house. She squealed and cowered in fear.

"Daddy, no, don't wanna go in there," she said.

"That's okay honey—we don't need to; there are plenty of houses around the corner," he said.

The father looked at the house, and his face showed a touch of fear as well. He grabbed his daughter's hand tightly and dragged her away, ushering the rest of the group along in his wake.

The boy watched their antics in confusion.

Once they were gone, he turned and stared at the house himself. There was nothing scary about the place.

It was a modest suburban house with a white picket fence in front with two small brick pedestals flanking the path and holding up the front gate. The grass was meticulously manicured, the trees trimmed to perfection. The garden path consisted of a series of pristine paving stones leading up to an inviting front door. Beside him, the front gate was freshly painted and shone brightly even in the diminishing light.

The boy shifted his weight around on the pedestal he sat on and looked up the street hoping to spy his mother. It was getting pretty dark, and he was surprised she'd left him alone for this long.

He picked out another chocolate bar and within a few moments was munching happily on nuts and chocolate.

The voices of another group wafted towards him. From this distance he was sure he recognised a couple of the boys from school, but as they came closer, he saw they were all about his age, but he didn't know any of them. That seemed very strange to him.

As they approached, they made no sign they'd seen him. The boy put it down to his lame costume. The group walked up and stopped right next to the gate.

The tallest of them pushed the smallest

boy forward, and one of them said, "Go on. Go up and knock on the door. See if you get some good treats."

The little one struggled against the others, terror filled his face.

"No, no, not the murder house, not the murder house. I don't want to end up the same way as Dylan did," he screamed. He managed to push backwards, slipped between the other boys' hands and bolted up the street.

They watched him go and the tallest boy shouted, "Chicken."

All of the remaining boys laughed for a few moments before moving away.

The boy watched them go while chewing on his chocolate bar and thought about what the little boy had said.

Dylan? he thought. I'm Dylan. I don't know any other Dylans.

He finished the chocolate then turned around to look at the house.

Everything had changed.

Now, the grass was long and dry, the trees overgrown and unkempt. The path made up of cracked pavers with dry grass springing up between them. The front door was a smashed mess of damaged wood. Every single window had boards up over broken panes.

Memories flooded Dylan's mind like he was watching his life play out on video.

The evening was bright. He walked down Oak Street with a bucket full of candy, happy with his haul, happy with himself. He stopped outside number 129. It was the last house before Palm Street and the last house he was allowed to trick or treat.

He grasped and opened the gate then walked up the pristine paved path. He reached the front door and rang the doorbell.

A kindly old man opened it, spoke softly to him and invited him in. His dream-self failed to see the eager grin on the old man's face and the way he peered around to check that no-one was watching.

The door slammed shut.

Dylan's ghost stood outside. The screams started inside.

He dropped his bucket of candy to the broken path and looked down at his hands. All he could see was the path below.

He realised his costume wasn't a ghost.

He was.

He began to cry.

First published in *Tricksters Treats #2* – Things In the Well Press, 2018

TRAVELLIN' LIGHT

By Bec Lewis

I see the ghost as soon as I board the number seventy-two bus.

He's sitting at the back—and he's staring right at me! It's enough to give you goosebumps.

He doesn't look like a ghost, I admit. Most of the passengers are schoolkids, so the pallid teenager doesn't stand out too much. But *his* sun-starved complexion didn't come from hours spent in front of a computer screen. This, I know.

Now he's checking out my trendy leather jacket. A lot of people do. He's wondering why a woman of my mature years isn't wearing a dusky pink, hip-covering anorak, I suppose.

I smile, but he looks away. No surprise there. I'm a member of the salt 'n' pepper brigade, a different species, according to his generation. For a moment I wonder if this was such a good idea after all. I don't want to see horror on his face once he finds out who I am. But he *is* the reason I got on the bus in the first place.

A man looks up from his newspaper and watches me head towards the back. "It's chilly up that end, dear," he says. "Heating must be off. Smells musty too."

"Whole bus feels chilly," his wife mutters.

I sit further along the back seat, leaving a gap between the ghost and me. He's wearing jeans and a green sweater. You'd think he'd relish the chance to dress in something ethereal, rattle some chains and be off somewhere scaring a schoolteacher. But no. Where's his sense of fun?

Time to break the ice. "Envious, huh?" I reckon that if I can talk in a snappy, modern way, I won't seem too grannyish.

"Sorry?"

I point to the other kids, most of them nodding to a tinny beat. "They have mp-pod-thingies—whatever they're called." Damn, I do sound old. "I noticed you don't."

"Never had one."

I know that, but I can't let on. Not yet. "I'm Mrs. Bowen." I extend a hand. Just testing. He doesn't shake it. He won't—or can't; I'm not sure exactly what ghosts *can* do.

"Peter." He turns to wipe his arm across the grimy window, carefully avoiding the words *"Travellin' light"* written in mirror-writing. Through the clear patch I can see we're passing the lake.

"Used to go there a lot, years ago," he

says.

"When you were little?"

"I was thirteen."

"You look about thirteen now," I say.

He doesn't redden at his slip. Ghosts don't, do they? "Maybe I look young for my age. I went there with my friend Cathy." He smiles. "We'd get into loads of trouble skipping school. We went exploring."

"Ah," I nod. "A different type of education."

He continues, "It's not as if we didn't catch up with schoolwork the next day. Her parents put a stop to it, though. They moved away, so I wouldn't be able to see her again."

"They didn't like her missing school."

I look away for a moment. "I expect they really wanted the best for her, wanted her to do well."

"But she was like me, she couldn't be cooped up. We understood each other so well." He sighs. "But I lived in a caravan, so even though I passed for grammar school, I was considered a bad influence."

"According to her parents."

"They couldn't see that Cathy needed to be free, like me. We even had our own motto, '*Travellin' light*.' We didn't want to be tied down."

"Just travellin' light, no ties, no rules, no baggage."

"Yeah." He looks surprised. "You're quite 'with it' for…"

"An oldie?" I put on a shocked

expression.

"No, er..."

"It's okay." I smile. So I'm old. But he *is* talking to me. And it's lovely to hear his voice after my husband's 60-a-day growl. I think back to a few days ago.

***

"My shirts aren't ironed," he'd said accusingly. "You been painting again?"

"Just a bit of drawing. My tutor said I need to get the perspective right."

"Your job's to look after me, woman."

"Ed, I need to practice." My voice had tailed off. I always knew it was no use arguing with him.

"Waste of time. You still driving to

your brother's?"

"Tomorrow," I'd replied and then in a flash of bravado added, "I suppose *you'll* be seeing Louisa."

I braced myself for a slap, but he just said, "Daft cow. I've told you—there's nothing going on." He smiled, but looking back, I think it had been a sneer.

***

The bus screeches to a halt at the roundabout, jolting me back to the present. I groan. "I hate buses."

"Me and Cathy used to love 'em. Her folks were well-off, so she'd pay my fare. We travelled all over, mostly in the holidays. But it was more fun when we skipped school."

"Sounds like a lot of fun."

"Oh, we were really living!"

I chuckle, thinking about two crazy kids dreaming of a life without rules, chores, and tellings-off. That dream isn't just for kids though, is it? "But you preferred travelling during school hours, because it meant you were breaking rules."

"It's as if you can see right through me." Peter smiles as he looks away, probably enjoying his private joke.

"What if I could?" I ask.

"What?"

"What if I could see through you?"

He doesn't get any paler. He can't. But I can tell he's shocked, by the way he's staring at me. I lean across the seat to whisper; no point in upsetting the other passengers. "You're a ghost. Aren't you?"

He gasps. "How did you know?"

"It was in the papers. Must be over forty years ago now. I'd just turned thirteen when it happened."

"That's how old *I* was."

"I remember the photos. Still the same ginger curls flopping over your eyes. Even though you're hiding your face with a cap, I recognised you immediately."

"No one else knows who I am. The paper said I didn't know what hit me. But I did—it was the number fifty-five bus. Saw it a second before it hit."

"Horrible." I shudder.

"You're wondering why I'd haunt a bus after being killed by one," he says.

"Most ghosts choose bricks and mortar."

"I lived in a caravan, remember?"

"Ah, yes," I say. "But even that's cosier than a bus."

He shrugs. "I'm a ghost. I don't do cosy. And I'm easier to find if I stay on the local buses."

"In case Cathy comes back." I wag my finger at him. "You're hoping she'd think of looking on the buses for you."

"Am I that transparent?"

We both laugh at his joke, and some passengers look round. "I can't think of any other reason for you haunting the buses," I say. "Peter, you do realise she'd be in her fifties now?"

"I guess. But true friendship lasts

forever. Doesn't it?"

"So you really don't mind that she'd be old by now?" I've already decided that if he does mind, I'll get off at the next stop. I guess that makes me a coward.

He shrugs. "Nothing either of us'd be able to do about that."

I could hug him. Except I probably couldn't. I don't know how these things work. "I know ghosts walk through walls. Can you do that fading away thing as well?"

"It comes with practice. You should see the look on people's faces when I do that!" He looks serious again. "Of course, it's not so much fun on your own."

"Peter, if you're always here," I say, "doesn't the driver notice?"

"If the bus is nearly empty, I dematerialise. I reappear when it's more crowded, staying at the back so I'm not noticed. Had to dematerialise a lot in the early years, otherwise I'd have been recognised."

He pauses and then says, "Why's it taken you so long, Cathy?" Just like that.

My voice comes out all croaky. "You knew it was me?"

"Not at first. After a while, maybe, but I wasn't sure."

"The years have not been kind, I know. I thought you'd be shocked by the way I look now."

"And I thought you'd be too grown-up to want to be friends again," he says. "But I always hoped, if you ever came back and spotted a bus with writing on the window, you'd find me."

"Ah, yes. *'Travellin' light.'* I knew you must be here when I saw that. Haven't liked buses since your accident, though."

"Why did you come back now?" he asks. "Visiting old friends? Lucky for me."

"I came here to look for you, Peter."

He frowns. "But I'm dead. You knew that, Cath."

"I knew you'd be floating around here somewhere."

"You didn't believe in ghosts when I knew you."

"No." I sigh, then say, "It's such a long time since those days. Somewhere along the way I guess I changed my views on a lot of things."

"I died the day after you moved, so my folks thought it was suicide. It wasn't." He reaches out as if to touch my hand but seems to change his mind. "Cathy, you never came to find my grave."

"My parents thought it best if I stayed away." Damn, I hate these awkward moments. "And then life got in the way. School, jobs, then marriage." I look at the floor. "But that's no excuse. I should have come. I'm sorry."

"Any kids?"

"I couldn't have them."

"I didn't know where you'd moved to," he says, "otherwise I'd have floated over to see you."

We both smile at this. "My parents didn't give me our new address before we moved," I say. "They didn't want me telling you. They wanted no further contact." The bus stops at the station and more teenagers get on. "I was going to write, though."

"I'm glad you're here, even though you're more like a mum now."

"Ouch." Best not to admit that I do feel sort of maternal towards him now.

He grins. "If only we could have fun, like in the old days."

"Even though I never came back, and even though I'm...?" I don't really want to remind him about my advanced years, but the words slip out before I can stop them.

"Age is irrelevant now. I'm a ghost, remember? And we're still friends, aren't we?" He frowns. "You got on without paying. The driver didn't notice, because of the queue, but *I* saw you."

"I can travel free now."

"But you're not old enough for a bus pass," he says.

"No."

"But you said..."

"Yes. These days, I travel free. I travel...*light*."

Amused, I look at the changing expressions on his face. First blankness, then confusion, and then the most beautiful smile as he finally understands.

"Cath, when?"

"Two days ago. My husband fixed the car. He'll enjoy the insurance payout, unless the police catch up with him. He'll probably marry his mistress. They've been seeing each other for years."

"Oh, Cath. You've been so alone. Like me."

"Not anymore, Peter. I've found my best friend again."

"You have." He puts on a mischievous expression, points down the bus towards the other passengers, and then whispers in my ear, "So let's liven this place up—before the bus starts moving. We don't want to cause an accident." He grins. "And then we'll visit your husband."

Following him towards the front of the bus, I feel like a girl again even though the staring passengers must assume I'm Peter's grandmother.

And when we reach the front we carry on walking—right through the windshield!

Twenty-five or more schoolkids start screaming. Giggling, Peter and I hover above the pavement for a few minutes, and then we start floating away to visit Ed. It'll be my first proper haunting.

First published in *Scribble magazine*, 2009

CHARLIE'S GRAVE

By Galina Trefil

The land was cheap. Maybe there was a reason for that.

A mass of old growth Redwood and Pygmy forest not far from the scenic Northern California ocean. No, this area wasn't the California that people portrayed in movies. The California of tanned and toned sun-bathers and surfers was decidedly several hours further south. This was Albion—a remote hamlet located in Mendocino County, the heart of the "Emerald Triangle." In a nutshell: drug country. These weren't woods in which one could take a casual stroll. When one lived here long enough, one knew not to ask questions. But eight-year-old Charlie's family had just flocked here from another state, hoping to build a new and better life. It wasn't long before he realized this wasn't a place like anywhere else…

Why was there a grave on the twenty-acre parcel which the family had just bought? Why hadn't the real estate agent even warned them that it was there, far back in the forest? Was this just the kind of thing that people around here took for granted?

The wooden headstone had long ago rotten away, obscuring the deceased's name, along with most of the other pertinent information about them. Vaguely, one could put a finger against the carved lettering and make out the remnants of a moss-covered prayer.

Charlie wanted to know who the grave belonged to. "It doesn't matter," his parents told him repeatedly. "Whoever is buried there died a century ago."

They were right. But, while this easily explained the decrepit condition the burial site was in, it in no way explained why someone had been buried up here in the woods, which had been almost entirely uninhabited at the time of the person's death.

"It's probably someone that used to live here on the property," Charlie's father, Frank, told him as he put him to bed. "You've got to remember, kid, that back then it wasn't always so easy to get to a respectable cemetery. The closest one over in Mendocino might've taken a few days to get to with a horse and cart. And, believe you me, that'd be one hell of a long few days. If the person died in the summer, the heat would get the body stinking real bad. The gasses inside the corpse might've made it expand and maybe, just maybe, even blow up." Charlie's eyes went wide at the visual image. "Oh, yeah," his dad nodded. "That happens sometimes. Even Old Henry VIII, when he was decomposing, he expanded just like a balloon until…POP! He wound up splattering all over the place." Frank chuckled, getting a morose rise out of the visual image. "Death isn't as neat and clean as they make it seem on TV, kiddo. Not by a long shot."

"Whoever buried them must have loved them very much," Charlie's mother, Rosemary, put in quickly, trying to soften the tone of conversation as she shot Charlie's father a disapproving glare. "That headstone may look terrible and broken now, but I'm sure that it took a lot of work to make. And, remember, back then everything was done by hand. What with the headstone, the boards, and the little picket fence surrounding it all, why, I bet it probably took months to make."

"Maybe a lot longer," Frank nodded. "Most of the paint's gone, but that grave's been out in the elements for over a hundred years…and you can still see the little flecks of white on some of it. Back in the 19th century, this whole area was pretty much logging camp country. Most people just had shacks and tents, really. Whitewash wasn't easy to come by. Something that lasted this long, well, it wouldn't surprise me if the purchaser had to get it shipped special all the way from San Francisco."

"Don't think of the grave as morbid, Charlie," Rosemary nodded. "Back then, people did the best they could in difficult circumstances."

"Heck, kiddo, back then you were lucky to get a grave at all. More likely than not, that person down there got wrapped in a sheet, got dug a hole, and the spot got marked with a stick or a rock. Everything else took time…But they're lucky that they had someone to care about them that much because, with all the drunks looking to get rich quick up here back in the day, I'd be surprised if there aren't dozens of bodies in the dirt that never got so much as a single word of God said over their poor, pathetic bones, let alone a proper burial."

"You think there's more dead people in the woods?" Charlie gulped.

Again, Charlie's mother glared at his

father. The man hesitated slightly, but then shrugged. "There could be," he finally replied. "But it's not a big deal. It's not like it really matters. Whatever's left of them got eaten up by bugs and animals a long time ago."

After his parents departed the room, Charlie heard his mother hissing at his father in the hallway. They were predictable words, such as how Charlie didn't need to hear about this stuff. His father insisted in turn that little boys loved the macabre and, if anything, it toughened them up. But Charlie didn't feel tough. He only felt more questions pulsing through his veins, along with a kick of adrenaline and dread that refused to let him sleep.

He was tired the next day at school in

Mendocino, a forty-five-minute commute one-way. He didn't fit in with the kids there. Mendocino kids treated Albion kids like freaks of nature and bullied them a lot, though Charlie couldn't grasp yet exactly why. To make matters worse, Charlie was pretty sure that his new teacher also didn't like him. "What's this?" she demanded, raising unnerved eyebrows as she held up the drawing he was making during art time. "Charlie, just what do you think you are doing?"

"Someone's buried behind my house," he mumbled quietly, wishing that her high-pitched disapproval wasn't so flagrant that it made the other students' heads turn in his direction.

"The assignment was to draw you,

yourself, with your friends! Why did you draw yourself putting flowers on a grave?"

Charlie shrugged. "All of this person's friends are dead. That means they need new ones."

The teacher glared, her shoulders hunching up slightly. "Did you know this dead person?"

"No."

"Then you're not their friend!" She scrunched the drawing into a little ball in her hands with such force that it reminded Charlie of cracking an egg. She threw the ball into the metal trash can beside her desk, cheeks burning with indignation. "Now do the task like I told you, or you'll get extra homework." She let out a deep huffing sound. "A grave! How disgusting!

What's wrong with kids these days?"

Later, when it was time to go home, Charlie retrieved his artwork from the garbage. Sitting on the school bus, he morosely watched his new environment go by. The ocean, the fields, the unending forest...It was all so overwhelmingly beautiful; beautiful enough to almost distract him from the questions that consumed him when he went home. Almost.

"Nutjob Charlie!" One of the other children taunted as the bus stopped, allowing several students to depart.

"Yeah," another one followed up quickly. "Charlie lives in a cemetery."

Well, great, Charlie fumed. Without doubt, that was going to be a popular rumour from here on out at school. As the aged bus driver, Hank, started the bus back up again, Charlie stared at his tattered drawing, cursing himself for making the image.

Hank drove the bus silently for a few minutes. He wasn't the friendliest of people, and he particularly hated being around all of these hyper little kids. As a result, Charlie was surprised when Hank addressed him now.

"You the caretaker's son?"

"Huh?"

"Rose Memorial Cemetery. Is your dad the one that stays on the property?"

Charlie shook his head. "If I really lived in a cemetery, don't you think you'd be dropping me off there?"

Hank shrugged. Charlie looked down at his picture. "Somebody's buried on our property. I shouldn't have let my teacher know. Now everybody's going to think that I'm weird."

"Oh, really? Who died?"

"I don't know…but I really want to."

"Don't the headstone say?"

"It's screwed up. I can't read it."

Hank went back to ignoring him, until it was Charlie's stop. Even after nearly two months of living here, Charlie still sucked in his breath when he knew that he was going to have to walk down the secluded quarter mile dirt road, labelled L, alone. Today, eyeing the yellow soil and thin, rough Pygmy trees which beckoned from the gaping jaws of L Road, Charlie felt the typical discomfort and longing for his parents to be there waiting for him. But they never were.

Reluctantly, he grabbed his backpack and slid it on. He was eight, damn it, he reminded himself; not a baby. There was nothing to be afraid of. Home was at the end of the road, not boogeymen, not monsters.

"You know," Hank called after him as he stepped out of the bus, "it could always be worse."

"Worse? What do you mean?"

"If there's really a grave on your parents' land, at least you know where it is. You know not to step on it. The dead don't like that, you know. If you step on a body, the spirit gets angry. You don't ever want to do that."

Charlie gulped, feeling almost like the drawing in his hand was burning into his flesh. Somehow, he feared, the grave could hear what Hank had just warned him about…and it wanted him to know that he'd been warned.

"Back in 1918," Hank noted, "there was an outbreak of influenza. It was one of the deadliest plagues in history—over fifty million people died, you know, and more than 600,000 of them were right here in the United States. The kids and the little babies especially couldn't make it. So many of them died that, up in Fort Bragg, at Rose Memorial, they got their own special part of the cemetery, back in the woods where the earth weren't flat. There wasn't room in the regular part to get them all buried, you see… And there wasn't time to get enough proper headstones made. Poor people couldn't afford to do that in a pinch, not with two or three or four of their little ones dying at the same time. So they'd put these cheap, tin little markers up over the children's graves… Geez, I tell you, there must've been a hundred of those crappy little markers sticking up out of the dirt back in the forest—a hundred, at least!

"But one day, I was up at Rose Hill, paying respects to an old friend. I saw that them markers weren't there anymore. Somebody, maybe the cemetery itself, maybe a hobo, hell, maybe some brats not much older than you, had come along and taken away every single little marker so don't nobody know them children's bodies are even there. So every time somebody takes a step back in the woods behind where all them rich people's graves are, what they're really doing is walking on a bunch of dead, little babies…and they don't even know it. Disrespect like that, though, intentional or not, it's got a price in the end.

"So you got a grave on your property, boy? Well, just you remember: could be worse, a whole hell of a lot of worse."

Charlie's lips parted in horror. Hank's craggy face sported a knowing grin and then he pulled the lever to slam the bus door closed. As the bus drove away, Charlie was enveloped in a cloud of dust that left him hacking and coughing. For just a moment, he was glad that the bus was gone. He didn't want the other kids to see how Hank's information was making his knees tremble.

"I hate it here," he whispered. "I want to go home." When he said it, he didn't mean home at the end of L Road, either. He meant "home" as in his home state. Mendocino County would never be his home.

He began to make the necessary trek towards his house, which would take him past the Pygmy forest patch that thickly clustered around where the burial site was. Most of the property was redwood forest, true enough, but the majority of L Road was made up of spindly, tightly-knit Pygmy trees. Their branches, to Charlie, seemed like soured, rotted flesh reaching out for him as their bodies strained to escape from the clay-like, solid soil beneath them. Despite their appearance, these trees weren't dead. They weren't that lucky. They were condemned, like patients in a rest home, to exist with the vaguest degree of life, while forced to jealously observe the distant redwoods, huckleberry bushes, and masses of rhododendron flowers which thrived and gloried in green and growing health.

When he eventually found himself standing at the spot in the road not far from the grave, Charlie stalled. Who would bury someone in Pygmy soil? Grass couldn't grow in it. Nothing but these scary trees could and it took them hundreds of years to reach the height of a human being. Charlie frowned, imagining the gravedigger standing at this site a hundred years ago—a body shrouded in the sun nearby. Would a shovel have successfully managed to penetrate that concrete-like ground? It didn't seem likely.

"He probably used a pickaxe," Frank ventured when Charlie arrived home and brought it up. "Or maybe the gravedigger just didn't bother to go down a whole six feet. Sure, it's the done thing, but this was the Wild West back then. People did as they liked. I wouldn't be surprised if the body is only two or three feet below the surface. Hell, maybe there was just enough of a hole to fit the body into, then the gravedigger covered it up and called it good enough.”

“It could be a cenotaph,” Rosemary put forward.

“What’s that?”

“A cenotaph, Charlie, gets put up when the dead person’s body has been lost. It’s comforting for people, even though they know the person’s remains aren’t really there.”

“That wouldn’t comfort me,” Charlie remarked quickly, scrunching his face. “But why put up a cenotaph in the middle of nowhere? Three miles away from town? Was Albion even a town back then yet?”

“The village dates back to 1844,” Rosemary nodded.

“You’d think that being around for this long would’ve moved the population up to at least two hundred people," Frank huffed.

"Oh, come on," she laughed. "There's two hundred people in the village. Nobody keeps records of just how many more of us live up here in the hills and in the woods."

"Yep," Frank snorted. "If a census taker walked out onto one of these properties, more likely than not, they'd be taking their life into their hands. You can't spit without landing on a heroin addict or pot-grower around here. Goddamn degenerates."

"Then why did we move here?" Charlie grumbled.

"Because when a giant mass of dopeheads live on valuable land, Charlie," his dad grinned, "all you have to do is wait. Give it enough time and they start to die off like flies. When one does, you can grab up their land at auction for beans. And that's what me and your mother did. There's a lot of crappy neighbours around here, sure, but give it time. They'll all keep pumping that poison into their veins and, in twenty years, they'll all be in the ground and all the properties in this area will be owned by nice, decent, respectable folk. Who knows? Maybe if Mom and I work hard enough, we'll be able to buy another parcel."

"What we've already got is good enough," Rosemary replied, shaking her head. "We don't need another property too."

"Good enough?" Frank laughed. "Oh, come on. A man can always use more land, Rosemary. Where's your ambition?"

Charlie looked at the floor, not sure how to react to his father's goals. "So the person who owned this property before us…they were a drug addict that died?"

"Damn it, Frank," Rosemary snapped. "Do you have to talk about this stuff with him? He doesn't need to hear it!"

Charlie's father hesitated, but then replied smoothly, "I don't know, Charlie. Don't really care either. Go to bed, kid."

Charlie skulked into his room, put on his pj's, and slipped under the covers. "Don't forget to say your prayers," his mother called to him through the closed door.

"Prayers," he fumed in response.

That night he awoke to…*scratch, scratch*…. Terrible, hungry sounds dragged across his window. Barely able to breathe, he remained perfectly still, eyeing the jet-black pane of glass. As wind and rain began to howl outside, the clawing noise only grew louder and more desperate to get inside.

Finally, Charlie couldn't take it anymore. He let out a high-pitched scream. He expected his parents to come running, but it was as if his thin walls were suddenly soundproof. He screamed again and again, but still, the only presence he felt was the terrifying intruder's.

He thought back frantically to all his moments at the grave. Had he ever stepped on it? Maybe he had and the angry spirit was coming for him!

Suddenly, a massive branch stabbed

through the glass, shattering it across the room, cutting red, dripping slices into Charlie's cheeks. Charlie jumped out of bed, hurling himself at his bedroom door. Hyperventilating and shrieking, he yanked at his doorknob. "Mommmmm! Daaaddd… Help meeee!"

Rainwater began to spatter the room at an alarming rate. A hissing sound penetrating his ears, Charlie flipped on the light switch. A middle-aged woman's face, pale almost to the point of being blue, loomed just outside. Her eyes, devoid of all color, glistened with tears as she leaned forward, scratching her own flesh raw against the window.

Charlie couldn't take it anymore. He fainted.

"Goddamn it, Charlie!" His father yelled at him first thing in the morning when he woke up. "What the hell is wrong with you? What did you do to your window?"

Charlie tried to explain.

Rosemary busied herself, applying antiseptic and bandages to Charlie's face. "He must have had a nightmare, Frank."

"Nightmare, my ass! He probably threw one of his toys—his baseball, maybe—and was too chicken to fess up last night. Look at all of this damage!"

"But, Dad, I screamed for you—"

"Just shut up!" Frank roared. "Shut up and get ready for school!"

Alone on the dirt road to take him to school, Charlie started to sob. "I want to go home!" he cried out. "I don't want to be here!"

But he didn't have a choice. He had to put one foot in front of the other, all the way to the end of L Road, and that meant passing the area again which so clearly belonged to a soul who, for all the efforts put into making it happy post-mortem, was very much yet unsettled.

When he got to the spot, he stood still for a moment, eyeing the dreadful woods. A woman's moan moved forwards through the trees, sinking into his ears. As if roots had sprung through his shoes, the petrified Charlie could not move an inch.

After a while, a sweaty young man appeared from out of the thicket, zipping up his pants. Unnerved to see Charlie standing there, he departed quickly without a word.

From the woods, gradually, a young female's singing began to trill.

Charlie debated his options for a moment. Clearly, the ghost had the ability to get him—had nearly done so last night. But maybe, just maybe, if he approached it, he could reason with it, make it leave him alone.

Full of terror, he bravely approached the grave. A blond girl sat on it, hooking her bra in place and then buttoning up her shirt. Red candles burned under the headstone, where strange little bones had been arranged. "Christ!" she shrieked, seeing him suddenly. "Where did you come from?" She swallowed. "What? Are you a peeping tom or something? Did you watch all that?"

"What are you doing?"

"None of your business, pervert," she snapped. "Get lost!"

"You're doing bad things to wake the spirit up, aren't you?"

She blinked, adjusting her clothes with palpable unease. "No," she replied quietly. "I'm doing bad things in order to keep him asleep. I'm paying my dues. Around here, we all have to."

"Him? You mean it's a man?"

She nodded, getting out a brush to fix her dishevelled hair. "Sometimes he wants things from people. There's no point in saying no."

"But the ghost can't be a man!"

Charlie snapped. "I saw it just last night and it was a woman!"

"You saw a ghost too?"

Charlie nodded emphatically. "It was a pale lady. She broke my window and did this to my face!" He tore off his bandages, revealing the ugly cuts.

The young woman swallowed. "I guess that you're going to have to find a way to pay your dues too, then."

"I don't understand."

"You're that new kid that just moved here?" He nodded and she let out a disgruntled sigh. "Well, welcome to the truth, then."

"What truth?"

"That the properties are cheap in Albion, but not for the reason that tourists think. It's because you never really own them. You can only pay rent."

"Pay rent to who?"

"To the dead. This is their land. This has always been their land. You do what they say or there are consequences. If one of them has it out for you, you had better figure out who she is and what she wants."

"How do I do that when I don't know where she's even buried?"

"The next time she comes to you, follow her. Maybe she'll lead you to her bones. It wouldn't be the first time it has happened around here."

"You think that I should just walk off into the forest and try to find a grave at random?"

"You do whatever you want to, kid.

You figure it out," she huffed, blowing out the candles and packing up her things.

Whilst Charlie stood staring at the gravesite, shivering at this new information, his parents stood looking down at their front porch.

"I don't know what to do about this new death fixation Charlie has," Rosemary mumbled.

"It doesn't mean anything," Frank shrugged, running his foot back and forth over the wooden planks beneath him.

"But what if he knows something? What if all those questions aren't really about that stupid old grave in the woods?"

Frank smirked. "You're being paranoid. There's no way he could know."

"But—"

"If Charlie found something out—it's not possible, but for arguments sake, let's just say he did, well, then we'll just pull him out of school. We'll tell everyone that he's being home-schooled. After a while, way out here, no one would ever notice if he..."

"If he what?" Rosemary frowned. "If he what, Frank?" she demanded.

He didn't answer her for a moment. Instead, he crouched down over the spot where he'd buried the house's previous owner. "It doesn't matter," he finally responded. "It's not ever going to come to that. Charlie doesn't and he won't ever know the real reason that we got this house. No one will."

Below his gaze, under the earth, a

vengeful mass of purification scowled. The steps which Frank and Rosemary had taken to properly conceal the corpse would soon be eroded by the winter rains, whose severity they had not planned on after the murder. The smell of death would find its way upward…and then, despite their initial belief, Charlie's parents would find this land could not be paid for cheaply. Unfortunately for him, so would Charlie.

YESTERDAY IS DEAD AND GONE

By Joshua E. Borgmann

1980s...

She said that she had always seen

them, but she never elaborated on any encounters from that bleak bastion of forgetfulness called childhood. Her stories always involved her as an adult encountering some phantom from her past. Her grandfather played a key role in many of these tales. She claimed to have been exceedingly close to him as a child; however, family sources suggest that this may have been exaggerated. The old man had certainly been around, but that this granddaughter had been anything more to him than any other grandchild during his time amongst the living cannot be substantiated. However, all of her family members agree she certainly made it clear that if she wasn't the apple of her grandfather's living eye, she certainly was his ghost's favourite.

She was never scared by his visits from beyond. She was quick to point out that he wasn't some undead beast that lurked behind her curtains or even some Caspar the Friendly Ghost want-to-be following her around the house while munching on spiritual popcorn. He just happened to show up at random moments. She'd be driving down the highway, and she'd see him beside her, and he'd tell her he missed her. She'd be butchering a goat in her yard, and he'd suddenly be standing next to her saying the beast would make for some good eating. She'd be arguing with the mayor at a town council meeting concerning the ordinance banning farm animals from residential areas, and he'd be sitting there telling her to give them hell.

During those early days of what we might call the pleasant hauntings, she also claimed to be visited by her Uncle Porky. Little is known about this man, and whether he was called Porky due to his weight or for some other unfathomable reason is a fact long lost. In fact, it is unclear exactly how Porky took on the title of uncle. Her mother had no brother, and the little that can be found about her father's side reveals nothing about a brother either. However, the woman's son has stated her mother had verified Porky's existence but little else other than the fact that he'd had a propensity for strong drink. As for what his ghost had to say, the woman said he was upset that "some dirty son-of-a-bitches" had thrown him in front of a train. The son did note that his grandmother acknowledged that Porky did work on the railroad and did meet his end under a train, but she claimed he had ended up there due to his own drunkenness.

The subject steadfastly stuck to the story that Porky never drank a drop in his life and certainly was done in by "those dirty son-of-a-bitches." However, she had little else to say about him aside from the fact that he had been her "favourite uncle," and his spirit often showed up to say, "How are you doing, girl."

Note: This researcher couldn't help but think of him adding "Give me some sugar," like Bruce Campbell in an Evil Dead movie.

1977

In 1977, the woman adopted her niece's son after the niece disappeared and the boy's father turned out to be a dead beat. However, the son never lived with her. She was known to be a hoarder and a crazy cat lady and apparently wished to spare the boy from this; therefore, she deposited him at her mother's house where he remained until leaving for college in the early 1990s. However, for the nature of this report, it is important to note that the son did have nearly daily contact with the woman. In particular, he often accompanied her on late night car trips to pick up her husband from work. As such, the son serves as a major source of information in this investigation.

1987…

The son identified the late 1980s as the time when a woman named Marie entered the subject's life. The son said he remembered Marie as an unmarried, elderly woman who had spent her entire life living with her father until he had died suddenly of a brain aneurysm a few years earlier. Marie and our subject first bonded over a cat Marie had taken in. The cat in question had apparently been one of the woman's cat hoard before inserting itself into Marie's much more peaceful environment.

Note: the son wasn't sure exactly how many cats the subject had at any given time, but he estimated the number at no fewer than twenty and no more than fifty. He noted that the numbers declined when she lost her own home and had to move into an apartment in the early 2000s. However, from the 1970s through the early 2000s, she lived surrounded by felines. The son states that she sometimes spoke of seeing the spirits of deceased cats as well.

Marie quickly became a fixture in the woman's life. In her, she found a fellow traveller with whom she could talk all she wanted to about ghosts, UFOs, evil prowlers, and warp zone holes. Plus, it didn't hurt that Marie had been battling cancer and needed someone to take her to doctor's appointments and grocery shopping trips, as well as help her with house cleaning tasks. Our subject applied and was hired by the State of Nebraska to fill this role, but Marie quickly became her best friend and joined her and the son on those late-night trips to pick up her husband from work.

The son described this time as a bizarre period when he sat in the backseat and listened to the two women jabber about warp zone holes that had taken hundreds of our planes during WWII and the increasing threat of snuff films, which they had been warned about by some late night conspiracy talk show. The son vividly remembered this was during the days of the so-called Satanic Panic when many idiots saw a cult behind every corner. He got a kick out of the women speculating about who might be in a cult because he fit the bill perfectly by being in love with horror movies and a huge fan of heavy metal bands like Slayer and Judas Priest.

Our subject also vented a lot about so called "prowlers," who she believed were breaking into or trying to break into her home. She claimed she would see them out of the corner of her eye, but by the time she got her shotgun, they were gone. She kept saying that if she ever caught them, she had a load of buckshot waiting for "the dirty son-of-a bitches." The son was amused because he didn't believe she had anything worth stealing, as all her possessions were coated in cat urine and shit. He said his "mother" and Marie were just two old bags of hot air.

He said every night was essentially the

same: pick up Marie, listen to paranoid babbling while Randy Travis played on the radio, pick up the husband, buy beer, listen to our subject berate the husband by calling him "a dirty son of a bitch," and ride down country roads looking for deer. The son noted that this activity should have been called "Nebraska Roulette" because deer are a true menace on the roads throughout the region, accounting for numerous accidents, yet our subject was going out of her way in the hopes of seeing some of them…every single night for over a decade.

As noted, Marie had cancer, and it seemed like her family was cursed, as at least half a dozen of her family members succumbed to the Big C before it finally embraced her for the final time in 1989. Marie's cat was summarily executed and buried with her.

Note: *The son wasn't 100% sure that the cat was actually buried with her.*

Some readers may wonder why Marie is being given so much attention in this report; however, that should become clear now that we have reached her death.

The son related the following tale:

Our subject claimed that she was driving home from the grocery store late during one of those Nebraska snow storms that pretty much obliterates one's ability to see even a foot beyond the windshield. She was driving along at twenty miles an hour when she thought she heard meowing from inside the car; however, she was sure none of her cats were inside the car. She took her eyes off the road for a moment but couldn't see a cat anywhere. At that point, she decided to turn up the radio, which she distinctly remembered was playing "Grandma Got Ran Over by a Reindeer," but the cat's meowing just got louder. She said she suddenly felt someone grab the steering wheel. She tried to stay in control, but the car swerved, and she saw a deer just beyond the front end of the car. She had no doubt that she would have hit it if the phantom hadn't grabbed the wheel. As she straightened out and continued down the road, she saw Marie sitting beside her, and her cat sat meowing on the dashboard.

A Note from the Son:

"You must remember that the woman was never stable. The whole ghost thing was only one small slice of the insanity that those of us who had the misfortune of calling her family put up with. She made all of us live in fear and made us dependent upon her. She was the only person in the family allowed to drive, and we lived twenty miles from a Wal-Mart or a major grocery store, so she had to be the one to take us for anything that we needed. She never let us forget how much of a burden this was on her. For example, I remember we were in the larger town one day. It was a few days after Christmas, and I had a Slayer tape I needed to return because someone had given me an extra as a present. I didn't think it was a big deal

because we were already in the area, so I asked her if we could stop at the mall so I could return it. Her hands tightened on the wheel when I asked, and after a few seconds she screamed, "I really wish I had a bomb to blow all of you son of a bitches to Hell." Everyone was a SOB to her. It made it hard to feel much love for her."

1996...

The son claimed she never stopped talking about ghosts, but it was mostly her grandpa or Marie and her cat that paid her visits for the next decade or so. He moved away to college but talked to her on the phone when required. According to him, he would have preferred not to talk to her at all, but he didn't have a way back and forth to college for holiday breaks unless she came and picked him up, so he had to play along until he finally got a driver's license some years later. He reported that she started talking about God and the devil a lot around his sophomore year. It was what he called "basic God Lord this…That Damn Satan that" talk for several months, but then she called him one afternoon and said, "Well, I've got a demon in my house."

She claimed she had been sleeping in her bed the night before when she was awoken by a couple of her cats "raising hell." She said that she knew it was more than a normal ruckus because the cats never woke her up.

"I thought it was another damn prowler," she said. "But then I saw the shape. It looked like a person, but it was small and pure black. I thought, maybe it was some black child that had broken in. Of course, folks around here don't let many of those kind live around here…They let the Mexicans and the Vietnamese come in with their damn talk everywhere…can't even read the signs in some parts of town, but our own black boys can't be around…No, the white trash bastards can't tolerate that…like they are any better."

When she stopped ranting, she went on. "So there was this thing standing there just as black as the ace of spades. I looked at it and said 'What do you want, you damned devil? You better just leave me alone, or the Good Lord will show you that he's the boss of you."

She said it kept standing there staring at her, so she dug around on her nightstand until she found her Bible, and she threw it at the entity.

"It went right through it, but the thing flickered and made a noise. I think it was a scream. I hurt it. But it wasn't no human scream…more like a cat getting its tail cut off. I knew right then that it was from hell."

The son asked her if it could have been a dream, but she wasn't hearing that. He states he mostly just went along with her because it was easier that way.

He reported that a few nights later, she called back with an update. She said that she had found a letter from a television minister in her mail the day before and had called some sort of prayer hotline hoping to speak with the minister. She was told the minister wasn't available, but they could help her if she told them everything. She did, and their solution was for her to read from the Bible every night and place it under her pillow. In addition, she should place a full glass of water by her bed to catch the demon. They also wanted her to send them $17.00 to get a vial of blessed water they claimed would send the demon straight back to hell.

The son claims that he urged her not to waste $17.00.

A few days later she called and left a message saying the glass of water had turned pitch black.

A few days after that, he received a second message saying she'd gotten the vial of water and confronted the entity.

The son says she never spoke of the entity again. Apparently, it did not return. However, she kept sending the minister $17.00 a month for the rest of her life.

Note: *I asked the son if she was a religious woman, a church goer. He said that she had never gone to a day of church in her life and believed that the only good ministers were on television. Everyone at the local churches were just a bunch of dirty son-of-a-bitches.*

2005...

The son recalled an incident that might reflect on later events:

"My great grandma died, but the rest of my family told me not to tell my adoptive

mom for a few days. She found out anyway because it was a small town, and gossip is the only business of a small town. Still, her siblings hid the funeral arrangements from her because they didn't want her there. It was kind of shitty, but she would likely have gotten in a fist fight with one of them if she had attended.

"She started talking about the television minster more after that. She also started claiming that my adoptive father was beating her in her sleep. Of course, he was five years in the grave by then."

2010...

According to the son, our subject stopped talking to him for a few years because he'd become too uppity for her.

He'd hoped to never hear from her again, but his hopes were dashed when she called and told him the television minister had personally called her and told her she was a special soldier for the Lord. He had told her that her gift of $17.00 a month was going to get her a big return real soon. He said he'd seen her packing boxes and that she'd be moving soon. This caught her attention because she was hoping to move to an apartment closer to the store, as she didn't remember her way around as much anymore. She said she'd gotten lost just the other day, but Marie's ghost appeared to direct her home. The minister told her she had a way with spirits and was truly his greatest disciple. He claimed to be a true prophet of the Lord and her personal messiah. She was a loyal servant, and a windfall was on its way to her. Her $17.00 would be rewarded.

Note: The son identified the minister as a popular prosperity gospel preacher who'd been dealing with charges of fraud for several decades. He was unable to verify if the conversation took place but several form letters from this individual's ministry were found among her things.

2012

She started leaving an increasing number of voice messages on the son's cell phone. The following are of particular interest:

5/12/12 12:30 AM

"The dirty son of a bitch is back. I told

him that he was dead and buried, but he just looked at me and said, 'Not anymore.' The damn devil must have sent him back to torture me."

5/13/12 5:00 PM

"I can't find that bastard father of yours anywhere. The son of a bitch ran off with that whore sister of mine last night, and they've been out drinking and running all night. I thought he was supposed to be dead, but he keeps showing up here, and now that dirty bitch is involved too. She's no sister of mine. You hear me. Not my damn sister, just a dirty whore chasing after men like a little girl when she's 75."

5/14/12 8:00 AM

"He got himself a car. I don't know how, but he pulled in here about three in the morning, blasting that damn Elvis Presley on the radio. Just as loud as could be at three in the morning and woke me up. He came in with my whore sister stinking of alcohol and hit me upside the head when I asked him what he was doing. He said that he could do anything that he damn well pleased since he was the one that was raised from the dead, and I couldn't stop him this time. That bitch just laughed when he hit me. You see, this is the kind of shit that I have to put up with. Pretty soon I'm going to call the law on the son of a bitch. I don't care if he is a ghost; the law will get his ass right good."

The next message was odd, even by her standards. It went on for so long that it eventually cuts off.

6/1/12 4:09 PM

"Something weird is going on. I don't know who is saying what, but I better not find out it was you, or I'll disown your fat ass just like that. You damn well better hear me and tell that bitch that you're married to that she better stay out of my business.

"Why the Hell won't my mom and grandma talk to me?

"Yeah, you heard me, and I'm not crazy. I know damn good and well what I'm talking about.

"I woke up this morning, and Mom and Grandma were already in the kitchen eating breakfast. I hadn't heard them even get up, but there they were, just sitting at the table eating toast and oatmeal. I asked them what was going on, but they just ignored me and kept on with whatever they were talking about. I hadn't been paying attention, but I started listening, and you wouldn't believe what I heard. They were talking about how I was nothing but a spoiled brat and that they should have beat my ass black and blue when I was little. That bitch mother of mine said that it was terrible how I treated that good man that I married and drove him to drink himself into an early grave. Grandma told her that the Lord was taking care of that, and the good man would be laughing in the end. It was his reward for putting up with me so many years. I couldn't believe that she would say that. I knew my mom was a dirty bitch, but Grandma was always good to me. I loved her.

"I'd had just about enough, and I asked them, 'Just who do you think you are, talking about me like that while I'm standing right here?'

"They didn't even act like they heard a word. They just kept on talking about how my sister had done okay even though her girls had given her trouble and her first man was a crook, but the Southerner wasn't too bad. They went on and on about why couldn't I be like her or like my brother, who had got rich working for President Reagan. They acted like I couldn't do anything, but my nasty ass brother and sister were so damned special.

"I yelled, 'This is my house. GET OUT!!!'

"But they just kept talking. Mom went

ahead and buttered another piece of toast and didn't even look at me, so I threw a coffee cup at her, and I swear to God, it went right through her.

"This doesn't make any sense. What have you been saying? I'm going to call the big minister man and he'll sick the Lord on you. You better…"

Message cuts off.

Note: The son stated,

"At the time of the message, my great grandmother had been dead for almost a decade, and my great great grandmother, the woman she called Grandma, died in the early 1970s before I was even born."

July 2012

The son stated that he received a call from the Grand Island, Nebraska, police department at approximately 11:15 PM on July 4th of 2012. He had just returned from a fireworks display, so he remembered the time fairly well.

His account follows:

"The officer told me that they had found my mother wandering in a Casey's General Store parking lot wearing a nightgown and house slippers. She said that she was looking for her husband. I alerted them that he was dead, and the officer said that he knew. He said that he had been dealing with several calls a day from my mom claiming that either her husband or the devil himself was out to get her. She also mentioned a sister who wouldn't leave her alone. I told him that the sister lived fifty miles away but hadn't spoken to her in years. He assured me that he had already spoken with her and that she wanted no contact with my mom. Apparently, she had said something like, 'that bitch could rot in a nursing home until I have the chance to spit on her grave.'

I asked the officer what he needed me to do, and he informed me that the officers who found my mother had concluded she was unable to state where she lived, but she had the keys to her apartment in her hand, so they had brought her home. Unfortunately, she claimed it wasn't her apartment. After hearing the address, I assured him it was. He agreed, as there were stacks of her mail all over the table and counter. Still, he asked me to try talking to her, as he was with her at the moment. I agreed.

She said, 'These damn fools brought me to the wrong apartment.'

'They told me that was apartment 17A,' I said. 'Isn't that your apartment?'

'Yes,' she screamed, 'but this isn't 17A.'

'The officer says it is. Look at the number outside the door and check.'

'Damn it, you're against me too. It says it is 17A, but none of my stuff is here. I don't recognize a damn thing. And where are my cats?'

I tried to remain calm, although I wanted to reach through the phone and strangle her. I said, 'You had to get rid of the cats.'

'Why the Hell would I do that.'

'The apartments wouldn't allow them.'

She huffed, 'That's some bullshit. I'd never live in a place without cats.'

'You didn't have a choice,' I sighed.

'I live in Wood River,' she bellowed.

'No, you moved years ago. You live in Grand Island now.'

'I wouldn't move around all the Mexicans and Vietnamese. You aren't my son. Who the Hell are you?'

At that point the officer took the phone away from her. I was told that she would be taken to a hospital for evaluation. Little good that did."

Note:

Records indicate that the subject called the Grand Island Police Department 72 times between May and August of 2012. Most of the calls were to report her husband missing or the presence of ghostly figures in her apartment. The police found nothing and deemed her a nuisance.

She was evaluated by a psychiatrist, psychologists, and several social workers. Some of these individuals thought she might be moving toward early stage dementia, but all deemed her lucid and capable of making her own decisions.

August 15, 2012

Message left on son's answering machine:

"They all came again. That dirty son of a bitch I was married to, my mother, Marie, Uncle Porky, my bitch of a sister, all my grandparents. Even all my dead babies…they weren't even born alive, but they were there too. Lots of cats, too, every one I had ever owned. He did all the talking while the rest of them circled me. He kept saying that it was time for a reckoning.

"'Your days are done. Your yesterdays are dead and gone. Today you face your reckoning.' He kept repeating that over and over.

"I told him that I had nothing to feel bad about, but he said, 'I'd learn.'

"They kept closing in on me, almost touching me. I kept hearing him repeat, 'Reckoning.'

"Please call; I'm scared."

The son did not call, and the subject was admitted to the hospital two hours later after being found wandering the streets in front of her apartment building screaming, "All my yesterdays are dead." Nurses at the hospital report that she kept mumbling, "A reckoning."

She died at 3:01 AM on August 16th. The coroner was unable to determine a definitive cause of death; however, there were no visible signs of advanced Alzheimer's. Her death remains listed only as natural causes. The doctors claim it was simply old age.

ABOUT THE PUBLISHER

BLACK HARE PRESS is a small, independent publisher based in Melbourne, Australia.

Founded in 2018, our aim has always been to champion emerging authors from all around the globe and offer opportunities for them to participate in speculative fiction and horror short story anthologies.

Connect

Website: *www.blackharepress.com*

Twitter: *@BlackHarePress*